JOAN HOHL

Double WOLFE

Silhouette Books

Published by Silhouette Books
America's Publisher of Contemporary Romance

SILHOUETTE BOOKS

DOUBLE WOLFE

Copyright © 2004 by Harlequin Books S.A.

ISBN 0-373-21827-3

The publisher acknowledges the copyright holders
of the individual works as follows:

WOLFE WINTER
Copyright © 1998 by Joan Hohl

WOLFE WONDER
Copyright © 2004 by Joan Hohl

Visit Silhouette at www.eHarlequin.com

Printed in U.S.A.

International bestselling author Joan Hohl
created one of romance's most memorable families
with her Wolfe dynasty. And now, Silhouette Books
is proud to present the bestselling novel,
WOLFE WINTER, along with a
brand-new Wolfe story, "Wolfe Wonder,"
together in one volume.

PRAISE FOR THE TALENT OF

JOAN HOHL

"Joan Hohl is a top gun!"
—*New York Times* bestselling author
Catherine Coulter

"Joan Hohl writes romance that
goes straight to the heart."
—*New York Times* bestselling author
Jayne Ann Krentz

"A compelling storyteller
who weaves her tales with verve, passion and style."
—*New York Times* bestselling author Nora Roberts

"Writers come and writers go. Few have the staying
power, the enthusiastic following of Joan Hohl.
That's talent!"
—*USA TODAY* bestselling author Kasey Michaels

JOAN HOHL

New York Times extended list and *USA TODAY* bestselling author Joan Hohl has written over forty novels and has won numerous awards, including the Romance Writers of America Gold Medallion Award and two *Romantic Times* magazine Reviewer's Choice Awards. One of the industry's most popular authors, Joan lives in eastern Pennsylvania with her husband and family.

CONTENTS

THE WOLFE FAMILY

Cameron Wolfe Sr. (d) m. Matilda "Maddy" Simmons

[4] Cameron
m.
Sandra Bradley

[5] Matilda — ***Lisa [6]***

[3] Royce
m.
Megan Delaney

Edward — Andrew — Tim

[2] Eric
m.
Tina Kranus

Mark — Todd — Brian

[1] Jake
m.
Sarah Cummings

Justin — Jeffrey

*** indicates twins
(d) deceased

1 — WOLFE WAITING
2 — WOLFE WATCHING
3 — WOLFE WANTING
4 — WOLFE WEDDING
5 — WOLFE WINTER
6 — WOLFE WONDER

WOLFE WINTER

To law-enforcement officers everywhere,
with thanks for their dedication and bravery
in the line of duty.

Chapter 1

The call came through ten minutes before the end of her shift, directing her to investigate a reported desecration of property at the new church just outside town.

Officer Matilda Wolfe—Matt to her family and friends—grimaced. Acknowledging the directive, she whipped the patrol car into a tight U-turn and headed north to the site of the crime. She did not activate the siren or the bar of flashers on the car roof; there seemed little point in doing so, since the late-night traffic was sparse and the perpetrator of the crime was probably long gone.

"Ten minutes," she muttered, her sharp gaze skimming the road before her and the bordering sidewalks; everything appeared peaceful and quiet, as it should at that time of the workweek night.

"Just ten lousy minutes," she continued her muttered grousing. The clustered buildings thinned, the area becoming more rural. "I'd have been back at the station, smirking at Uncle Jake, my venerated chief, while my replacement was making this run."

Feeling somewhat better for having vented her annoyance, Matt steered the car onto a blacktopped secondary road, and allowed a soft smile to ease her tight lips.

The smile was in response to her thought about the man who was her chief, and her uncle. Jake Wolfe was at the station unusually late, having gone in after being notified of the apprehension of a rape suspect.

Her uncle had started as a rookie patrolman with the Sprucewood Police Department over twenty-five years ago, when the town was a lot smaller and the police force consisted of only a handful of men. He had worked himself up through the ranks as the town and the force had grown and expanded. Jake had made chief two years before Matt had graduated from the police academy and joined the force.

At that time, Cameron, Matt's father, and the eldest of the four Wolfe brothers, and a special agent for the FBI, had been, and still was, bureau chief of the Denver office. He'd held that position since before his marriage to Matt's mother, Sandra.

Along with her paternal grandmother, Matilda, for whom Matt had been named, her uncle Jake and his wife Sarah, had happily assumed the role of surrogate parents of Matt while she attended the police academy.

Recalling her early days on the force, Matt laughed aloud. Her uncle Jake had been tough on her, tougher than he'd been on the other rookies. But he'd done so only because he demanded the best from her, expecting her to uphold the family tradition of excellence and dedication to law enforcement principles.

While Matt had suffered moments of resentment for being judged by such high standards, passing the rigid Wolfe mettle test had endowed her with the satisfying rewards of self-esteem, value and worthiness.

Matt was a good cop—a darn good cop, and she knew it. So did everyone else.

She had earned the unqualified respect of every member of her family; aunts, uncles, cousins, but most importantly, her parents and her sister, Lisa, who had followed their mother into the practice of law.

The thought of her parents, her sister, sent a thrill of anticipation through Matt. She would be seeing them soon, as her parents and Lisa were coming east in a few weeks for the holidays.

Another thought made Matt grin. Along with having earned the respect of her entire family, she had earned the right to smirk at her chief on occasion.

The thought was more warming than her police-issue leather jacket.

A few minutes later she reduced her speed to a crawl, then made the sharp turn onto the curving driveway leading to the church that had been built just a few years before. Its profile gleamed stark white in the glow of the spotlights strategically positioned in the grounds.

Bringing the car to a stop, Matt took note of a dark shape emerging from the shadowed church entranceway. The figure was male, and large. As she stepped from the car, she slid her hand to the holstered police-issue pistol strapped to her waist.

That is one extremely tall woman.

The Reverend David Macdonough—Mac to his friends, and most of his parishioners—made the observation while watching the uniformed .woman stride toward him. Gliding a swift but comprehensive glance over her imposing length, Mac judged her to be some four or five inches shorter than his own six feet four-and-a-half inches. Which placed her at close to six foot.

Oh, yeah, she was tall, all right, he reflected, feeling a little jolt as she moved from the darkness into the glare of the spotlights. Tall and shapely and drop-dead gorgeous.

Admiring the spun gold color of her hair beneath her regulation hat, Mac extended his hand as she came to a halt a prudent distance from him.

"Good evening," Mac said, offering her a smile as he took a careful step closer. "I'm David Macdonough, pastor of the church. I placed the call to the station. Sorry to have had to bring you out here so late, and on such a cold night, Officer…"

"Wolfe," she readily supplied, removing her hand from the weapon at her waist to grasp his in an unsurprisingly firm grip. "And responding is my job, sir, time and cold weather notwithstanding."

Mac liked the sound of her voice. It was low, kind of throaty, with a sexy hint of smokiness. He liked the feel of her hand, too, the strength beneath the softness of her skin. He felt regret, along with a tingling sensation, when she slid her palm from his.

"The report said there's been an act of desecration," she said in brisk tones. She raised golden, delicately arched eyebrows over eyes that appeared to be the exact shade of dark, rich chocolate.

"Yes, that's correct." Brought back to the reality of why she was there, Mac suppressed a sigh. Turning, he indicated the crèche set up off to the side of the walkway in front of the church.

"If you'll follow me?"

To the ends of the earth.
Startled by the errant thought, coming as it had on

top of the jolt she'd experienced by the touch of his hand, Matt compressed her lips and trailed after the right reverend across the frost-stiffened lawn.

Why in the world would she have felt that electriclike zing from his hand against hers, or had such a thought about a stranger? Or any man, come to that. It was a new experience for Matt—and one she felt she happily could live without.

She wasn't interested in feeling intrigued by a man. Matt had grown up in a family of law enforcement officers. She knew, better than most, the constant fear *their* life partners lived with every day.

When she had taken the oath to the force, Matt had added another oath to herself—that of walking her chosen path alone, without the emotional baggage of a constantly concerned husband or significant other.

And she certainly didn't need the distraction of a zing of awareness now. This particular man was an ordained pastor in the bargain, Matt upbraided herself, her now-wary eyes measuring his impressive figure.

Of course, he didn't look anything like her idea of what a minister looked like; he certainly didn't look anything like her pastor. That gentleman was elderly, almost fragile in appearance, thin and rather smallish.

The Reverend Macdonough was the exact opposite of elderly, fragile, thin and small.

Matt's trained eye swept from the top of his head to the running shoes on his big feet. Six-five, she decided, and approximately one hundred and eighty pounds, give or take a couple of ounces. And, unless she missed her guess, precious few of those pounds were made up of fat, but pure toned muscle.

He wasn't bad to look at, either, if one found attraction in a dark-haired man with a harshly hewn bone structure, a long, thin, aristocratic nose, sculpted lips, and piercingly direct dark blue eyes.

"—as you can see."

The deep syrup-over-shrapnel sound of his voice snagged Matt from the mists of reverie. Fortunately, his pointing finger showed her the damage inflicted, sparing her the embarrassment of having to ask him to repeat the first part of his remark.

Oh, yes, Matt could definitely see, and the sight instilled in her both a feeling of sickness and a flash of outrage.

The crèche was constructed entirely of wood, from the cradle to the attending figures to the stablelike shelter in which the figures of the Holy Family were set. The figures themselves appeared to Matt to have been cut from one-half- to three-quarter-inch plywood, and were scaled slightly larger than life-size. They stood well over six feet tall, most likely, she figured, to be clearly seen from the road. The paint on the flat surfaces used to depict clothing and facial features had been applied by a steady hand, and a talented eye for detail.

The single figure in the scene not constructed of wood was that of the child. The infant Jesus was represented by a toddler's soft-skinned baby doll. It had been lovingly wrapped in a large woolen shawl—probably belonging to a parishioner or the pastor's wife, Matt mused. She ignored a disquieting sensation instilled by the likelihood that the reverend was married.

Collectively, the crèche was a beautiful and reverent piece of work, worthy of admiration and praise, not wanton vandalism.

After years on the Sprucewood Police Force, Matt had witnessed many scenes of destruction, the results of violence, the aftermath of accidents of all kinds. She had reacted to those scenes with revulsion for the sheer stupidity of it all.

But this…this scene before her had a different, deeper effect on Matt. Her sense of outrage stemmed from an inner spirituality unrelated to any particular religious belief or denomination.

Appalled, a sadness constricting her chest, Matt stared for long silent moments at the figure depicting the Virgin Mother. A protest rose in her throat against the hate that had directed some obviously disturbed person to obliterate the Virgin Mary's face with flat black paint.

"Sickening, isn't it?"

"Why?" Matt wasn't even aware of giving voice and substance to her despair and confusion.

"I've asked myself the same," the Reverend Macdonough murmured. "You can't help but wonder what's going on inside the head of a person who could do that."

Matt slanted a glance at him and discovered his expression reflected her feelings. The Reverend Macdonough was experiencing a similar confusion and despair.

No life had been wasted. No innocent had been defiled. No person had suffered physical damage. And yet, on some level, the desecration was almost frightening.

A gust of cold December night wind shivered through the surrounding evergreens. The chilled air drew Matt from her spiritual anguish and back to the reality of her purpose here.

"You've not touched anything?" She shot another, sharper look at the pastor.

He shook his head. "No, of course not. And I didn't walk up to it for a closer look." His smile was wry. "With the frost, there should be footprints."

Matt agreed with a brief nod, relieved that the man of the cloth appeared to possess some practical intelligence.

"There probably won't be much evidence to go on," she felt duty-bound to admit. "A dash to the figure, a few quick blasts from a can of spray paint, and then a hasty retreat.'' Sighing, she turned from the unsettling scene and headed for the car. "I'll toss the ball into the lab crew's court, then tape off the area."

To Matt's surprise, the pastor matched his long stride to hers.

"Can I be of assistance?" he asked in response to her questioning glance. "It's getting colder, and we could cut the exposure time in half."

"Thanks but..." She paused to catch her breath as another gust of wind smacked her square in the face. Pulling the car door open, she dove inside, grateful for the warmth blasting from the heater of the idling car. She was reaching for the two-way when the pastor slid into the passenger seat.

Eyeing him, she flicked the button on the control. "Four-one," she said, identifying herself to base.

The two-way crackled. "Go ahead, four-one."

While making her report, Matt avoided looking at the silent man next to her by staring at the dashboard. Her gaze settled on the digital clock; a groan vibrated her throat; she swallowed it. Groaning would not change the fact that she should have gone off shift thirty-five minutes ago.

"So now what?" he asked after she had finished and replaced the handset. "The tape?"

Matt angled her head to gaze at him. "Yes, the tape first."

"And then you'll have to interrogate me?" Amusement gleamed in his eyes.

"I'm afraid so, sir." Her tone gave clear indication that, though she respected his profession, she would follow procedure. "Sorry."

"No need to be," he assured her. "I do realize that, for the moment at least, I am a suspect."

His approval rating went up a few notches on Matt's personal judgment scale. The Reverend Macdonough was neither arrogant nor a fool, believing himself above the law because of his profession.

Thanks to the surrounding trees, and the pastor's assistance, the taping-off went swiftly. Still, feeling the bite of the frigid wind, Matt was chilled to the bone by the time they finished. She was both relieved and happy to turn the scene over to the lab crew when they arrived a few minutes later.

She turned to the pastor, but before she could voice her first question, he offered an invitation.

"Would you like to step inside, out of this wind? That's my place, over there." He indicated a house set a short distance to the side of the church. "I don't know about you, but I'm freezing."

"Well…" Matt slanted a glance at the lab crew, fully aware they didn't require her presence. "There's no rule that says you can't have a hot drink while interrogating someone, is there?"

"No, there are no rules against that…so long as the drink is nonalcoholic," she said, smiling.

He smiled back. "Wouldn't dream of offering alcohol to an officer on duty," he said, striding off toward the house. "Come along," he called over his shoulder, "before we both freeze fast to the ground."

The house was neither large nor small, but average. Though of good quality, the furniture was decidedly masculine, a lot of leather and wood. There were few adornments, knickknacks and the like. Yet it had a welcoming ambience, and was deliciously warm.

"Oh...feels good," Matt murmured, rubbing her cold-numbed fingers.

A quirky smile tilted the pastor's lips. "I noticed a pair of gloves on the seat of the car," he said, a teasing light springing to life in his eyes.

Matt gave a careless shrug—at least she hoped it looked careless. Considering the flutter his gleaming eyes had activated in the vicinity of her heart, she wasn't sure she had pulled off the careless appearance.

"I seldom wear them," she admitted, breathing easier when he turned away, motioning her to follow. "They're too bulky," she went on, trailing him into the kitchen.

"Hard to hold a police issue .38 with fingers stuck inside lined leather, huh?" His voice was serious in contrast to the dancing light in his eyes.

"Something like that," Matt agreed, averting her eyes as she dug a notepad from her pocket.

"Coffee, tea or hot chocolate?"

Matt glanced up, and felt her breath catch in her throat. Heavens, she thought. For a man of the cloth, he has wicked eyes.

"What's your pleasure?"

Matt was tempted—sorely tempted—to find out if she could shock and rattle him with an outrageous response, but she quashed the impulse.

"Hot chocolate, please," she said, sticking with propriety, and wondering why she'd been tempted in the first place. "If it's not too much trouble."

"No trouble," he said, opening a cabinet above the stove and removing two packets of the mix from a box. "Take off your jacket and hat and have a seat. This will only take a few minutes in the microwave."

"Thanks." Placing the notepad and pencil on the table, Matt removed her hat and set it next to the notepad. She shrugged out of her jacket and hung it over the back of a chair, then settled on the seat.

Hands folded on the tabletop, she watched as he prepared the two cups of hot chocolate, appreciating his efficiency. His spare, competent movements reminded her of her father and uncles—four men fully domesticated by a shrewd mother.

A gentle smile curved her lips.

"Pleasant thoughts?"

His question scattered the memory clouding her mind. "Hmm," Matt hummed, nodding. "I was thinking about my family...my father."

"I like that." His voice was warm with approval. Smiling, he set a steaming cup of hot chocolate in front of her, then circled the table to sit opposite her.

"You like...what?" Matt frowned.

"The sound of your voice when you said 'father,'" he said, raising his cup to his mouth for a tentative test taste.

She laughed. "How did it sound?"

"Oh..." He shrugged. "Warm, loving...with perhaps a hint of longing."

"They're in Colorado."

"'They'?"

"My folks," she explained. "My mother and father, and my sister."

He took a swallow of the chocolate drink, studying her with contemplative eyes. "They're on a winter vacation?" he asked.

Matt gave a quick shake of her head. "No, they live there, have since before I was born."

"And yet, you're on the police force here, in Sprucewood, Pennsylvania," he said, a frown drawing his dark brows together.

"Hmm," she murmured around the chocolate sip she'd taken into her mouth.

"Might I ask why? I mean..."

Her soft laughter silenced him. "I know what you

mean," she said when her laughter subsided. "But it's not as puzzling as it may sound." She took another sip before continuing. "My father is originally from Sprucewood. His mother still lives here, as does his youngest brother. I spent most of my summers here while I was growing up." She grinned. "And I like it here."

He grinned back at her. "So do I."

"You're from around here originally, too?" Matt asked, figuring if he could probe, she jolly well could, too; she was a cop, wasn't she?

"No." He shook his head. "I was born in Virginia, but I've lived all over the world." His smile was wry. "My father was a career serviceman—marines."

"Was?" She raised an eyebrow. "Retired?"

"No." His expression and voice were somber. "Deceased. He died from injuries from a car accident."

"I'm sorry." The sentiment seemed inadequate, but what else was there to say?

"Yeah, me, too." He sighed. "We lost my mother to cancer the year before."

Matt felt terrible, knowing how devastated she'd feel in the same situation. "That's...awful."

"For me...yes," he said, his eyes bleak. "But, in truth, I had already lost my father. The life had gone out of him before the accident—he just seemed to fade after my mother passed away.''

"Too bad," Matt murmured, somehow knowing it would be the same for her father in the unthinkable event that he should lose her mother. The mere thought sent a chill down her spine. She hastened to change the subject.

"My father is a career law enforcement officer." Her smile was tentative yet wry. "FBI."

"Whoa. Impressive," he said, lifting his cup to drain the last of his drink.

Matt couldn't tell from his tone of voice whether or not the reverend was being facetious, but she kind of suspected he might be. So, just in case he was, she decided to impress him a little bit more...then get on with her interrogation.

"Not really," she said, coolly insouciant. "You see, law enforcement is something of a Wolfe family tradition. Other than my grandmother and my aunts, we're all in some form of it."

"All?" His drink finished, the reverend leaned back in his chair and stretched his legs out under the table, looking for all the world as if he were settling in for a lengthy discussion. "How many law enforcement Wolfes are there?"

Matt was tired. She still had her reports to fill out before she could go home, and she felt certain her captain would rip a verbal strip off her for taking so long on this assignment. Nonetheless, since she had offered the tidbit of information about her family in the first place, she thought it would be unfair not to respond.

"There are eleven of us working on the front lines, so to speak, and two behind the lines," she said, stifling the need to yawn.

"Eleven..." He looked astonished, then frowned. "Would you care to sort them out for me?"

"Another time, perhaps," she answered. Pulling the notepad toward her and picking up the pencil, she gave him her most professional, no-nonsense look. "Now, I think we'd better get on with the interrogation."

He muttered something she didn't quite catch, something moreover that she felt certain she had misunderstood.

"I beg your pardon?" she said, convinced she had to have misunderstood, because it had sounded to her like he had said, "Dammit to hell." Nah, she decided, she was tired, that was it.

"Don't have much to tell," he said, the corners of his lips again twitching with that quirky smile.

Something about that smile bugged Matt. Her spine growing rigid, she gave him a drilling stare. His expression was benign, innocent. Hmm, too innocent, maybe? she mused.

"Are you planning to begin anytime soon?"

"What?" Matt frowned.

"The interrogation," he reminded her, his ex-

pression now somber and serious. Although a spark
of that wicked light still gleamed in his dark blue
eyes.

"Oh, yes, of course," she said, advising herself
to get a grip. "How did you happen to discover the
act of desecration?" she asked briskly.

"I was returning home from visiting a parishioner," he began when she interrupted him.

"The parishioner's name?"

He gave a name, a female name. Hmm, Matt
thought again as she jotted down the name. Then,
shoving speculation aside, she said, "Go on."

"Right." He nodded. "If you noticed, the driveway leads from the road, then up to and around the
side of the church, where it branches into two lanes.
One leads to the parking lot in back, the other to my
garage."

Matt's brief nod indicated that she had noticed.
How could she not have?

"Well, when I drove by the crèche, I caught a
glimpse of something that didn't look quite right,"
he said.

"So, after I parked the car, I walked back along
the drive for a closer look." He moved his broad
shoulders—Matt couldn't help but note their
width—in a light shrug. "And that's about it." He
smiled. "I will confess I was tempted to walk up to
the figure, touch it to see if the paint was still fresh

and tacky…" His smile widened. "But I resisted the temptation."

"Commendable of you." Matt favored him with a dry-as-dust look. "And that's when you called the report into the station?"

"Yes."

"Could one of your parishioners be nursing a grudge against you, or be disgruntled with church policy in general?" He frowned.

"It's possible I suppose," he admitted. "But I believe I'd be aware of it if someone did. I know them all fairly well, at least the ones who regularly attend services. The congregation's not very large."

"Do you have any known enemies—some person or persons seeking to strike at you?"

"No." His shook his head. "As stated, I'm relatively new to the area." A wry smile tugged at his very masculine and attractive lips. "I haven't been around here long enough to make that sort of enemy."

"No one knows you well enough yet to hate you, huh?" she drawled.

"That's about it." He laughed. The deep, rich sound having a strangely exciting effect on her.

"Okay." Matt flipped the notepad closed and pushed her chair away from the table. Rising, she settled her hat on her head and shrugged into her jacket. "If you should think of anything else, or if you notice any suddenly odd behavior or attitude in

one of your parishioners or personal friends, let us
know.''

"Certainly, although I can't imagine either a
friend or parishioner committing such a wanton
act,'' he said, plucking his jacket from the back of
a chair.

Matt gave him a quizzical glance, but started for
the front door.

He was right behind her.

"Will you keep me apprised of any progress you
make?'' he asked, following her outside.

"Yes.'' Matt started walking, and frowned when
he stepped to her side. Sure of his intentions, she
angled a sidelong look at him.

"Your lab crew has left,'' he said by way of an
explanation.

"So I see,'' she murmured. "Still, it's not necessary for you to escort me to the car, Reverend
Macdonough.'' She lifted her right hand to brush her
fingers over the butt of her holstered pistol. "I can
take care of myself.''

"I'm sure you can.'' He ran a telling glance over
her tall, imposing—some might say, intimidating—
form. "And the name's David,'' he said, smiling.
"Or, if you like, Mac. Most people call me Mac.''

"Hmm,'' she hummed, by way of avoiding com-
mittal or reciprocation.

Reaching the car, she grasped the door handle,
hesitated, and then turned to bid him good-night.

He didn't return the salutation. That quirky smile was back in place at the edges of his mouth. ''What do most people call you?''

''Officer Wolfe,'' she said, deadpan, pulling the door open and sliding behind the wheel.

He laughed aloud.

''Good night, Reverend Macdonough.'' Matt shut the door, fired the engine, released the hand brake and set the car in motion, backing around to head down the driveway to the road.

The deep, rich, disturbingly exciting sound of his laughter reverberated inside her head all the way back to the station.

Matt didn't like it…because she found it much, much too attractive, and him much too stimulating. And the very last thing she wanted was to find herself stimulated by or attracted to him, or any man, for that matter.

In Matt's belief, and oft-stated opinion, she was better off walking the law enforcement road alone.

Chapter 2

He'd slipped again.

His laughter dwindling to a lopsided smile, Mac ambled back to the house. His smile changed to a fleeting grimace as he passed the crèche.

Why? he asked himself, heaving a sigh. Why would anyone…

His thoughts fractured. Why wonder why? There were people in the world, disgruntled, disturbed, and flat out fanatical, that was why.

Mac knew, better than many, about people like that. He knew more than he wanted to know. Serving in the Armed Forces' Special Services had given him an in-depth education on the aberrant mental workings of a whole spectrum of different peoples.

Hadn't someone once said that it took all kinds?

Well, Mac had seen all kinds. The observations had finally gotten to him.

Hadn't someone else said something about man's inhumanity to man?

In the line of duty, Mac had stood witness to the truth of that saying. His service time had toughened him, hardened him, and in the end, sickened him, in mind and spirit, tested his innate belief of the ultimate goodness of the species called man.

A child shall lead them.

In the end, that prophetic verse had borne bitter fruit inside Mac.

Mac had experienced his crucible on sight of the large, imploring eyes of a small child. The poor mite had been rendered to the point of starvation by the deliberate acts of the greedy and ruthless leader of the child's ill-used and confused people.

Thoroughly disgusted with the world in general, Mac had done what, for him, previously would have been the unthinkable. He had quit, simply walked away from responsibility, duty, pride.

After first wallowing in the sins of the flesh, freefalling in a downward spiral until hitting rock bottom, the quitting had eventually proved to be the path of his salvation.

While losing himself, Mac had found redemption. Cleansed and strengthened by renewed belief, and armed with a sense of purpose, he had set about putting himself back together by cleaning up his act.

The struggle against his own inner demons was now five years past.

But Mac still had moments when he slipped...as he had earlier, with his impulsively muttered remark to Officer Wolfe.

The lopsided smile was back in place when Mac reentered his house.

Yes, he had slipped with the muttered, "Dammit to hell," but... Mac shrugged—off the remark and out of his jacket at the same time.

He had felt frustrated by her reluctance to give him a rundown of her various family members involved in the business of law enforcement.

Mac even acknowledged why he'd felt frustrated. He was interested, but not from an overriding curiosity about her family. In truth, he had felt an immediate interest and attraction to the woman herself.

Bemused by the self-realization, Mac went about the business of clearing away their hot chocolate mugs. He secured the house and prepared for bed with his usual, if absent, efficiency.

It had been some years since he had experienced so much as a glimmer of interest in a woman, let alone a twinge of physical attraction.

His disinterest had had nothing to do with the tenets he had embraced upon his salvation. His church, his denomination, did not demand abstinence.

Mac had been celibate by choice ever since his emotional enlightenment and emergence from the depths of degradation over five years ago.

His own personal, earthly savior, that incredible person who had been the means of Mac's salvation, though compassionate and sympathetic, had adhered to the principles of tough love.

Mac, compassionate and sympathetic, as well as understanding, also practiced tough love in his dealings with his fellow humans. But he practiced the hardest on himself.

Not once throughout those years of abstinence had he been visited by the allure of sensual temptation.

Until tonight, on sight of Officer Wolfe.

Weird.

Lying on his back in his bed, Mac stared at the shifting patterns of moonlight on the white-painted ceiling of his bedroom. He contemplated the stirring desire quickening his mind and body.

After so many years the sensation felt strange— not unpleasurable, just strange.

And he didn't even know her given name.

Strange indeed.

Mac's eyelids felt weighted, and they slowly drifted shut. Yet his mind remained active, dissecting this startling phenomenon of attraction.

In this case, "phenomena" perfectly defined the condition, he mused. For he felt the attraction on different and distinct levels.

There was, of course, the physical level, and Mac's attendant discomfort. Yet there were clear indications of interest on an intellectual level, too. In the brief amount of time spent in her company, Mac had detected elements of Officer Wolfe's sharp intelligence and keen wit.

And there was an emotional level, as well; the deep, abiding emotion of family love. The note of unqualified love in her voice when she'd spoken of her family—her father, her mother, her sister, and who knew how many others—had struck a deeply buried chord inside Mac. He was achingly aware of being without family or close friends, a man alone in the world.

A soft sigh escaped Mac's guard, breaking the silence of the cold night.

Though in a secret place inside him Mac would always mourn the loss of his parents, and then his younger sister, his only sibling, in a fiery auto crash, as well as the subsequent loss a few years ago of his benefactor and mentor, he seldom gave a thought to being alone in the world.

His faith, all-encompassing and comforting, had sustained him. It had strengthened him, accompanied him along the path he had freely chosen to follow.

While accepting the sorrow of personal loss, Mac had not felt bereft of the loss of the bonhomie of close, personal friendships or the intimacy inherent in relationships with members of the opposite sex.

Even with Corine Baxter, the still young and pretty widowed parishioner he had visited earlier that evening, Mac had not felt so much as a hint of an attraction, physical or emotional. Even though he couldn't help but notice that she had sent out unmistakable signals of a personal interest in him, he simply was not interested. He hadn't been in a long time.

Until now.

The stirring intensified in the lower regions of Mac's body; he shifted in a fruitless attempt to ease the discomfort.

Why? Mac frowned. There were lots of whys scurrying around inside his head.

Why now?

Why her?

Why not?

A faint smile of amusement tickled the edges of his mouth—self-derisory amusement. After all this time, the reactivation was almost funny. But not nearly funny enough to distract his mind from the acute discomfort of his body.

Unbidden, and unwelcome, considering he was trying to decrease the ache, not expand it, an image of Officer Wolfe grasped control of his mind and senses.

With amazing clarity, Mac could see her as clearly as if she were standing at the foot of his bed...or lying beside him on top of it.

His imagination re-created a tormenting picture of her as she had appeared seated beneath the glare of the kitchen ceiling light. Her delicate features had been cast in stark relief, the creamy smoothness of her skin accentuated by the hundred-watt bulb inside the frosted globe of the ceiling fixture.

And her hair…after she had removed her hat, her hair, brushed back and twisted into a knot at her nape, was tawny in color, shot through with shards of gold.

Mac felt a sharp, intense desire to see her hair freed from that knot, to curl his fingers into the silky gold-streaked mass.

He flexed his fingers, and half groaned, half laughed at himself. Sighing instead, he ordered his brain to continue its mental examination of her.

Free of lipstick, her lips were a tempting pink, ripe-looking and luscious. And her eyes were the exact shade of dark rich chocolate. Deep and inviting.

Her androgynous uniform could not conceal the allure of her full, high breasts, the enticing curve of her narrow waist, slender hips, rounded bottom, and below.

Below. Mac unconsciously heaved a yearning sigh. Even with the concealment of the straight-legged pants, it was obvious that her legs were long. Never having seen them, he just knew her legs were those of a kind to set a man's imagination, and libido, into overdrive.

He sighed again. Overall, his imagination revealed the tall form of one very appealing and sexy woman.

And a sexy-looking woman who appealed to him was the absolute last person he needed to encounter at this particular juncture of his life. He had dedicated himself, his life, to his mission of salvation.

A shudder ran down the length of Mac's body as a groan of protest rose to lodge in his throat and echo inside his head.

Why her?

Why now?

Why me?

Even while the questions plagued his brain, Mac attempted to distance himself from the physical torment by concentrating on the amusement factor.

It, too, would soon pass, he assured himself...and then, he would laugh.

"I'm home, Gram," Matt called, pulling the kitchen door closed behind her and shutting out the wind.

"About time, too," Maddy Wolfe called over the sound of the TV set. "You get an assignment right before quitting time?"

Matt smiled as she removed her hat and slipped out of her jacket. This wasn't the first time she'd felt grateful to be living with someone who understood the demands placed upon the life-style of a police officer.

"Yeah," she answered, unbuckling her gun belt as she walked into the living room. Setting the weapon on an end table, she crossed the room to the white-haired woman ensconced in a flower-patterned, wing-backed chair. "Ten minutes before quitting," she went on, bending to place a kiss on the woman's lined but still soft cheek. "Can you believe it?"

"Of course, I can believe it." Her smile soft and loving, Maddy patted Matt's hand. "In the early years, before he was promoted to sergeant, your grandfather was often assigned to investigate right around quitting time." Her smile sad with memory, she flicked off the TV. "Come to that," she went on, smothering a yawn as she rose from the chair, "things didn't change all that much after he moved into the narcotics division."

Matt felt a sympathetic pang in her chest for her beloved grandmother. After all these years, Maddy Wolfe still mourned for her husband, who had been cut down during a drug bust, giving his life in the line of duty.

Maddy straightened to her full height—just a few scant inches shorter than Matt's own six feet. Her grandmother, now in her eighties but with the vigor of a woman twenty years younger, sighed with acceptance.

"I'm sure your father, your uncles, and every one of your cousins has put in their share of overtime." Her smile turned teasing. "So don't go feeling like the Lone Ranger of the force."

Matt laughed, as she always did each and every time her grandmother offered the same advice.

Maddy laughed with her, then covered another yawn. "Well, now that you're home safe, I'm for bed." She raised her eyebrows. "Unless I can get you something to eat, or a hot drink?"

Always the caregiver, Matt thought, shaking her head. "No, thanks, Gram. I had a cup of hot chocolate a little while ago." Feeling, for some incomprehensible reason, unwilling to explain how she had come by the hot drink, she quickly added, "I'm bushed. All I want is a shower and my bed."

"Then I'll say good-night." Maddy turned and started from the room. "Sleep well, dear."

"I will."

After a soothing hot shower, Matt stepped into sleeping shorts, pulled on an oversize T-shirt emblazoned with the promise Chocolate Cures Curious Cravings, and burrowed beneath the covers.

Sighing, she let her body relax and closed her eyes, certain she'd be out within seconds. And she might have been—if a vision hadn't swirled, then settled in, firing her imagination.

Against her will, an image of David Macdonough formed front and center on the stage of her tired mind.

Go away, Matt thought on a silent groan.

The image smiled at her, displaying a flash of white teeth in concert with a blaze of blue eyes.

Lord—but he was good to look at.

The admission was as good as a declaration of surrender; the image settled in for a long visit.

Captive to her own imaginings, Matt examined the vision with her inner eye. Resentful of her captivity, she searched for surface flaws.

There weren't many. Oh, perhaps his jawline was a mite too squared, too hard-looking. And yes, maybe his lips were too defined, the line too set in determination. But, other than those...

Face it, Matilda Wolfe, he appeals to you, she told herself, reluctantly surrendering to the sheer male attractiveness of David Macdonough.

That wicked light sprang to life in the blue eyes of the image, that sensuous light she felt positive didn't belong in an ordained minister.

But, ordained ministers were men. Human. With all the frailties of the species. Weren't they?

The question brought a sigh. Matt felt much too tired to theorize on the basic humanity of those who had felt the calling. She was too wary of the pull on her senses by an individual who had apparently heard the call.

Yet it was there. Whether she liked it or not her attraction for David Macdonough was strong, physical, and emotional in nature.

And Matt didn't like it.

Go away, she thought again, blinking.

She felt both surprised and chagrined when the image vanished.

Then it was the inner conflict that kept her awake.

Considering the few hours' restless slumber she received, Matt was not her usual bright-eyed and bushy-tailed self when she began her shift early the next afternoon.

Reading the report from the lab crew's assessment of the church merely abraded her already chancy mood.

The crew had verified the paint was of the spray variety of a well-known brand that was readily available everywhere. They'd also found a couple of toe imprints from hard-worn sneakers. The size of the imprints indicated the sneaker wearer was either a child or a small, thin adult.

A child? Matt thought with dismay as she studied the brief report.

Naturally, after four years of wearing the badge, Matt knew full well there were kids, some appallingly young, who angrily and willfully wreaked havoc and destruction on humans as well as inanimate objects.

For Matt, it was heartbreaking because the majority of young offenders she had dealt with had committed the random acts in a desperate cry for help.

On an intellectual level, Matt accepted the fact of a young person's capability to commit acts of physical violence and vandalism. But emotionally, she cringed at the very idea that a young person would think to desecrate a religious symbol.

In a perfect world, children would be lovingly cared for and protected, their innocence inviolate until they'd had a chance to grow and mature.

Grow up, Wolfe, Matt impatiently told herself, sighing as she set the report aside. Sadly, the real world was far from perfect.

Come to that, she reflected, settling her hat on her head and waving an absent goodbye to the desk sergeant before exiting the station, the opposite seemed to apply.

She heaved a sigh as she slid behind the wheel of her patrol car to begin her regular rounds. On really bad days, Matt had the scary feeling the human race was hell-bent on a downward spiral into chaos.

Her normal optimistic outlook dimmed by deprivation of sleep and her depressing ruminations, Matt viewed her route with less than her usual enthusiasm.

The day was as gloomy as her thoughts; overcast with clouds the particular odd shade of gray that threatened snow before nightfall.

Thankfully, this was the last day of her shift and

she would have two whole days free before starting another. Actually, her off time amounted to three days. Her first day back would be Sunday, and she'd be working the dead-man's shift so she wouldn't have to report in until midnight. The thought of her approaching downtime was the one bright spot on the otherwise dark terrain of Matt's mind.

Brooding, Matt made the turn off the blacktop country road onto the church driveway without conscious decision.

She frowned; then shrugged. What the heck, she mused. Since she was in the vicinity, she might as well stop, relay the lab report to the reverend, and ask if he had thought of anything that might help.

As excuses went, it was as good as any other.

Telling herself wryly that self-deception was a fool's pastime, she brought the car to a stop on the driveway near the crèche site.

The figure of the Virgin Mary had been restored to its former beauty. Not a trace of the marring black paint remained. A satisfied sigh whispered through Matt's lips. The careful hand of the artist had wrought a loving serenity to the delicate features.

Her spirits lifted by the restoration, Matt drove on to the parsonage. Stepping from the car, she started for the house. The front door opened before she was halfway along the walk.

"Good afternoon, Officer Wolfe." The Reverend Macdonough was every bit as appealing in the light of day as he had been the previous night. Truth to tell, he was even more attractive...in a rugged, rough-hewn way. Matt's spirits ratcheted upward another notch.

"Afternoon, Reverend Macdonough," she returned the greeting, and his welcoming smile.

"Mac...or David...please." His smile chided.

Matt hesitated, then gave a brief nod. "All right, David, if you insist."

"I do." He waited, one eyebrow hitched.

She sighed. "Okay, David, my given name is Matilda..." Her eyes narrowed at his quickly concealed surprise. "My friends call me Matt."

His gaze swept her form, from the flat top of her cap, to the mirror-shine on her shoes. A slow smile teased his lips—and her nerve endings.

"You don't look like a Matt," he observed in a dry-voiced drawl. "But you don't look much like a Matilda, either."

"What, exactly, does a Matilda look like?" Her voice matched his for drawling dryness.

"Somebody's grandmother," he responded at once.

"Bull's-eye." She laughed. "That somebody is me. I was named for my father's mother."

"Mmm. And she's already got the nickname Matty...right?"

"Maddy," she corrected. "And, since Maddy and Matty are too similar, I got stuck with Matt."

"Ah...now I think I understand."

"Understand what?"

"Why you chose David instead of Mac," he explained. "Mac and Matt are also too similar, right?"

"Yes, of course."

"Uh-huh." He nodded, obviously suppressing a grin. "How about a cup of coffee...Matt?"

"I'd appreciate it...David."

Stepping back, he swung the door wide and invited her inside with a sweeping movement of his arm. As she moved past him, Matt caught a whiff of his scent, an intoxicating mixture of tangy citrus and healthy male.

Her reaction to his distinct smell was both confusing and unnerving. For an instant, Matt felt lightheaded. A hollow sensation invaded her stomach and robbed the strength from her legs.

What the heck! she thought, locking her knees to remain upright. She had never...until now. Must be because her stomach was empty. But, telling herself her response to him was caused by the lack of nourishment, and believing it, were altogether two different matters...especially after the night she'd spent.

Her movements stiff, she entered the house, then paused, waiting for him to precede her.

"Kitchen okay?" he asked, cocking an eyebrow.

"Fine." She wet her lips; shivering in response to the intent stare he fastened on her mouth.

"Thirsty?" David's voice was low, husky-sounding. His eyes were dark, hooded.

"Y-yes." Rattled, her throat suddenly parched, bone dry, Matt swallowed.

His steady gaze monitored the convulsive motion of her throat. When he raised his eyes, the darkness was gone, replaced by a speculative gleam.

"Are you...upset about something?"

"No." Matt shook her head, too quickly, too hard. "No, I'm fine, really." It was a lie; she wasn't fine. She felt odd, jumpy, as if every nerve ending was quivering in anticipation of...something. Why? She was afraid she knew...and that rocked her inner peace.

He arched that same eyebrow again, only this time it had a quizzical slant.

If her behavior puzzled him, which it appeared to do, she couldn't blame him. She felt every bit as confused as he seemed to be.

"Did you have lunch?"

Matt blinked, thrown by the suddenness of his question, the briskness of his voice, and the correctness of the conclusion he had reached. Without delving into the possible reason for it, she answered at once, and with complete honesty. "No." She wasn't about to admit that she'd had no breakfast, either. She opened her mouth to inquire as to why he'd asked, but he didn't give her time.

"That's what I figured." A half smile quirking

his lips, David turned away. Striding into the living room, he called to her. "Come along, Officer Matt, I'll give you something solid to go with your coffee."

Chapter 3

Matt felt like a fool. Holding her spine rigid, she fought an urge to bolt from the house, from his presence. She trailed behind him, her reluctance evident in her slow, stiff and measured steps.

"Have a seat, Matt. Relax, it's no big deal." Although David was standing at the kitchen counter, his back to her, his advice came through loud and clear.

But it was a big deal, she silently argued, sinking onto a chair and frowning at his back—his broad, muscular back. Not understanding what the hell was happening to her—or what it was all about—*made* it a big deal. An extremely big deal.

Finished fiddling with the coffeemaker, he walked

to the fridge and swung open the door. "Want to share a cheese and mushroom omelet?" He turned to face her, eyebrows raised, expression hopeful.

"Yuck." She shuddered.

"You don't like eggs?"

"I love eggs."

"You don't like cheese?"

"I love cheese."

"Ah, it's the mushrooms."

"I hate mushrooms."

He grinned. "It's heavy-going here, but we are learning things about each other."

Talk about your big deals, Matt muttered silently. Keeping the thought to herself, Matt decided to pass on his remark. "I'm really not very hungry, David, but I would love a cup of that coffee."

He shifted his gaze to the glass carafe. "It's not finished yet. How about a sandwich?"

She shook her head.

"If you missed lunch, you should have something." He arched that eyebrow. "A toasted English muffin? I've got cranberry," he added as inducement.

"I'm on duty, you know," she reminded him, making a show of glancing at her wristwatch.

"It'll only take a minute to toast a muffin." He thrust a hand into the fridge and pulled out a long container in a plastic sleeve. "I'll just pop one into the toaster for you," he said, prying apart two muf-

fins and dropping them into a four-slot toaster. "You
need nourishment to perform your duty to the best
of your ability."

Matt rolled her eyes, but didn't bother protesting,
certain it wouldn't do her any good anyway. She was
the authority here, wasn't she? So when had she lost
control of the situation?

While she was trying to figure that one out, David
poured coffee into two cups. The muffins popped up
in the toaster as he set a cup in front of her.

"See that?" He grinned. "Perfect timing."

Perfect teeth, too. And flashing to advantage in a
perfectly demoralizing grin. The observation created
a hollow feeling inside Matt.

At that moment David set a plate with two steaming, aromatic halves of muffin next to her coffee cup.
The scent of cranberries blended with the healthy
male aroma of him, activating her taste buds.

For the muffins…or for him? Shocked by the
thought, and the curl of sensuality it caused deep
inside her, Matt felt weak with relief when he moved
to take the chair opposite her.

"Thank you, it smells wonderful." She forced
herself to look up at him, and felt the bottom fall
out of her stomach. He looked so…so…appetiz-
ing.

"So do you."

Matt jolted, alarm streaking through her. Had she
spoken aloud? Or had her expression reflected her

inappropriate thoughts? He was a minister, for goodness' sake, a man of the cloth.

"Smell wonderful, I mean," he clarified—to her undying gratitude. "Your scent is light, enticing. Not heavy with musk or the badly combined and overpowering, funereal fragrance of flowers."

His observation of scents so closely paralleling her own, Matt was struck speechless. She simply stared at him—gaped, actually, since her mouth was already open in preparation of taking a bite of the muffin.

"Yes?" David prompted, obviously expecting a comment of some sort from her.

Matt's mouth snapped shut. She shook her head. "Nothing…it's just…" She shrugged.

"Well, that certainly clarifies everything." His voice held a droll inflection; his eyes laughed at her. "It's just…what?" he persisted.

"It's just…that…well, it struck me as odd. I mean, your opinion on scents is so similar to mine…it just seemed…strange, somehow, er—" Matt broke off, floundering in her own inadequacy. Was she babbling? Yes, of course she was babbling. Dammit. What was wrong with her? She never babbled.

The laughter she had seen lurking in his eyes escaped from his throat. The wholly masculine sound of it danced on the air and down her spine.

For an instant Matt teetered on the fine line between offense and amusement.

Amusement won. A smile tickled her lips, then quickly expanded into a chuckle.

"I sound like an idiot, don't I?"

He shook his head, getting himself under control before responding. "An idiot? Not likely. You sound human, with all the frailties entailed." He valiantly fought back another bout of laughter. "You do such an excellent job of projecting the image of the stern, no-nonsense officer of the law, that it's a relief—a revelation—to discover the woman inside the cop."

His explanation left her stymied, groping for a response, and refusing to acknowledge a sudden need to know what he *thought* of the woman inside the cop.

"I like her."

Matt caught herself just in time to keep from revealing the shock wave his remark set off inside her. Was she so transparent? Once again he had appeared to read her like an open book, and she didn't like it, the sense of vulnerability it instilled. Besides, cops weren't supposed to wear their thoughts on their expressions, for everyone to peruse.

"You really don't know that woman," she said, rather pleased with the repressive tone she'd inflected into her voice.

"But I'm beginning to," he countered. "I know she doesn't like heavy, cloying scents. I know she does like chocolate, and coffee, cranberry muffins, eggs and cheese..." He smiled. "And I know she does not like mushrooms."

"Food preferences." Matt flicked a hand in a gesture of dismissal. "Fragrances."

"And I also know," he continued, his voice soft, intense, unaffected by her dismissive tone, "that she can feel deeply affected by the senseless desecration of a religious symbol."

Too close.

He was getting too close, Matt thought, tamping down an edgy sensation. She must be slipping. It wasn't good, safe, for anyone to be able to read her so accurately—not even a man of the cloth.

Most particularly *this* man of the cloth.

But David had, however unwittingly, offered her the means of redirecting the line of conversation. She could turn it away from her; personally, and to the reason she was there in the first place.

Yeah. Right.

Ignoring the unsubtle nudge from her conscience, Matt polished off the muffin she couldn't remember eating, or tasting, then got to the business at hand.

"That was good, thank you," she said. "But it really wasn't necessary. I only stopped by to tell you the gist of the report from the lab crew."

For an instant his expectant expression was altered by a flash of something. Disappointment? Then it was gone, replaced by a look of interest, and the raising of both eyebrows, leaving her strangely excited, pondering the portent of that fleeting expression.

"Did they find anything that might be helpful to the investigation?" he prompted, his intent gaze probing *her* expression.

"Not much," she said too quickly. "The paint was a well-known, common brand," she continued, instilling brisk professionalism into her voice. "But you were right about the ground. They were able to retrieve footprints." She sighed. "Unfortunately, all they found were toe marks left by worn sneakers, the size and indentation indicating a small, thin adult...or a child."

"A kid?" He revealed another flicker of emotion, clearly pained, before his eyebrows drew together in a frown.

"Kids have been known to commit random acts of vandalism with spray paint, you know."

"Of course, I know," he snapped, giving her a mild shock with the show of impatience. "Being a minister does not necessarily equate with naiveté, Officer Wolfe. Because of the very nature of our work, we pastors deal with all kinds of aberrant behavior."

Well and truly chastised, Matt inclined her head in silent acknowledgment of his claim.

"It's not much to go on, is it?"

Grateful to him for letting her off the hook, Matt shook her head.

"No," she said, pushing her chair back and rising. She shrugged into her jacket.

"Could they get a make on the shoes?"

"Yes, they did. The shoes are a brand sold in discount stores." She settled her hat on her head, and gave him a tight smile. "The kind kids call Bobos."

"And could have been purchased in any number of places," he concluded.

"Right." Matt nodded.

David exhaled a sigh. "A tough one."

She nodded again, then arched her eyebrows. "Unless...you can recall one of your parishioners— one who might be dissatisfied about something— who fits the 'small, thin' description?"

He thought about it a moment, then slowly shook his head. "No...as I said last night, offhand, I can't think of anyone, small and thin or otherwise."

She sighed; there really wasn't much to go on.

"You could stop by, check out the congregation," he suggested. "You never can tell, you might pick up on something. You're trained to recognize unusual behavior, aren't you?"

Matt ignored the latter to question the former. "Stop by? You mean for church services?"

"No. You're always welcome, of course," David

was quick to assure her. "But I had a more informal atmosphere in mind...like the supper for instance."

She frowned. "The supper?"

He nodded. "The Christmas craft and cookie sale, followed by the spaghetti supper," he explained. "The church has it every year at this time."

She looked blank; he laughed.

"You had to have seen the sign while on patrol." He chuckled. "It's too big to miss."

"The sign," Matt repeated. Then the light went on. "Oh, you mean the sign along the road, right off the end of the driveway."

"The very same," he concurred, lips twitching with amusement, eyes laughing at her.

Matt was getting pretty darned tired of feeling foolish. Her spine grew stiff; her voice grew frosty. "Yes, I noticed it. I just didn't read it. When is this event to take place?"

"Saturday—one to whenever." He hesitated.

"Of course, people may react to the uniform." He shrugged. "But by then the church regulars will be aware of the incident, so they shouldn't be too surprised."

"I'll be in street clothes—since I'll be off duty on Saturday."

"You'll stop by?"

"Yes." Matt smiled. "I might even bring my grandmother with me. Gram loves church socials, and eating out. And spaghetti's one of her favorites.''

"I'll be looking forward to meeting her," he said, sounding as if he really meant it.

"Hmm," Matt murmured in her unconscious, habitual, judicious-sounding hum. "Now, I must go." She turned and headed for the door.

David was right behind her. "Afraid they'll put out an all-points on you?" he drawled, striding around her to open the door.

"No. They know where I..." Her voice faded as she moved to the door. "It's snowing."

Big as half dollars, the lacy white flakes looked like tiny ballerinas swirling on the breeze.

"Beautiful, isn't it?" David murmured, stepping out to stand beside her. "Not laying yet," he said, sweeping a glance over the ground. "Must have just started."

"Beautiful, yes," Matt agreed, sighing. "But if it continues, it'll make a lot more work for me." She slanted a smile of acceptance at him. "I'll probably spend my shift chasing fender-benders." With a light shrug, she walked to the patrol car.

"Drive carefully."

Matt paused in the act of swinging open the car door, surprised by the seriousness of his tone. She glanced over her shoulder at him, a mocking smile on her lips.

"I'm always careful, Reverend Macdonough,"

she said, her voice tinged with a note of warning. "I'm a very careful person...in and out of the car."

"Prudent," he said, nodding. A spark of understanding flared to life in his eyes, baffling Matt. She wasn't certain she understood what, exactly, she was warning him about.

Time to retreat, she advised herself, pulling open the door and sliding behind the wheel. A thought occurred as she flipped the ignition, firing the engine. She rolled down the window and stuck her head out.

"About Saturday," she called to him. "What if there's an accumulation of this stuff?"

"Unless it's up to your tush, the social's on," he said, grinning at her start of surprise.

"Uh-huh," Matt muttered, switching on the windshield wipers, then releasing the hand brake. "Then I suppose I'll see you Saturday."

"I'm looking forward to it."

Innocent enough response, Matt mused, steering the car along the driveway at a sedate speed. Yet there had been an underlying something in his tone that had sent a thrill tingling down her spine.

What was that all about?

Frowning, Matt brought the car to a stop at the road at the end of the drive, to stare, as if mesmerized, at the back and forth swish of the wipers. She spun her mental wheels, trying to figure out what had so unsettled her about those innocuous fifteen minutes or so she had spent in the parsonage.

And it had been innocuous. Nothing remotely out of the ordinary had happened to cause this churned-up sensation inside her. Nothing.

Strange.

And yet, Matt had to admit that from her first sight of him last night stepping out of the church, she had experienced an unusual reaction to him. And that reaction had remained in play, keeping her edgy and restless throughout most of the night.

In fact, she felt a curious, quivery and inexplicable excitement just being in David Macdonough's company.

And maybe she had just hit on the answer. Being in David Macdonough's company.

The man unnerved her, simple as that.

Or, perhaps, not so simple at all.

By a mile, David Macdonough was the most attractive and interesting man she'd run across. And good looks alone had nothing to do with it.

Matt knew plenty of flat-out handsome men, men with smoother, less rough-edged good looks…a few with the added attraction of wealth. Yet, not one of those men had ever made her feel shaky inside, overwarm, even in the winter cold, foolish, and too alive.

The tingly thrill tiptoed down her spine once again, causing a delicious little shudder.

David was a minister, she sternly reminded herself. A man of the cloth.

Forbidden fruit... Wasn't there some old saw about the most tempting fruit being—

"Four-one?"

Matt blinked, jerking alert at the summons from the two-way. Get it together, Wolfe, she chastised herself with chagrined impatience, reaching for the handset and depressing the call button.

"Four-one," she replied.

"What kept you?" the dry voice of the dispatcher, Dina Marsden, asked in an inquisitive drawl.

Matt was nothing if not scrupulously honest. "The reverend invited me to have a cup of coffee and an English muffin while we talked."

"What flavor?" Dina's voice had gone from dry to wry—with a hint of laughter thrown in.

"Cranberry." Matt's lips quirked.

"Yummy. You cops have all the breaks," Dina muttered. "Are you back on patrol now?"

"Yeah." The quirk worked its way into a grin.

"Oh, goody."

Matt waited, thirty seconds. Then she sighed. "You got something for me?"

"Yeah," Dina returned sardonically. "Check out a vehicular accident at the intersection of Chestnut and Willow Run. No reported injuries—just a lot of shouting and accusations flying back and forth."

"I'm on it." Flipping the call button to off, Matt replaced the handset. As she pulled onto the road, she spared a quick glance at the big sign, reading it aloud as she slowly drove past.

"'Annual Christmas Craft and Cookie Sale. Spaghetti Supper To Follow. Everybody Welcome.'"

Matt grinned again, adding, "Even cops."

Chapter 4

*D*avid.

Bemused by the distinctive, smoky sound of her voice saying his name echoing inside his head, Mac watched the squad car until it was lost to his sight around the curve in the driveway.

He liked the sound, liked the warm sensation it generated deep inside him. There were only ever two people who had called him David—his soft-spoken, gentle mother, and the tough-talking woman who had picked him out of the gutter and saved him from himself.

And now, Officer Matilda Wolfe chose to call him David rather than Mac.

A portent? Mac didn't know, nor really care. All

he did know was that he liked it…and her. Matt turned him on, an amazing feat, under the circumstances.

A large, delicate snowflake came to rest on his left eye, and tangled in his lashes.

Smiling, he brushed the moisture away, then stared up at the leaden sky.

Was that a blessing or a condemnation, Sir? Mac asked, addressing his Maker in his usual method of silent communion. *After all these years of my disinclination and disinterest in the opposite sex, do You approve or disapprove of this unexpected and unsought reactivation of my libido?*

There was no answer from above, no rumble of thunder, no streak of lightning.

Mac hadn't expected such a display. Grounded within his faith was the belief that mankind had been endowed with a reasoning mind for the purpose of applying it. What was the point, otherwise?

In effect, at least for Mac, his answer was in the point, and the point was crystal clear: each man— and woman—had to think for themselves.

There were guidelines, of course, writ in stone by a finger of fire.

Having embraced those guidelines, Mac adhered to them…and there was not one *Shall Not* pertaining to a single man's interest in a single woman.

But was Matt Wolfe a single woman?

Mac frowned at the thought. He had noted many

things about her person and personality, but, off-hand, he could not recall if revealing rings had adorned the third finger of Matt's left hand.

Unconcerned with the wet stuff pelting his face, Mac continued to stare at the sky, deciding he'd take it as a good sign if it turned out that Matt was not only single but unattached.

Ah, the mental games we mortals play, he chided himself, shaking his head at his own frailty.

Nevertheless, Matt did turn him on.

And, after all these years, Mac rather enjoyed it.

Shivering, he turned to reenter the house, hoping the snow wouldn't amount to much because now, even more than before, he was anticipating the church social.

For Mac, Saturday couldn't come fast enough; but, in the meanwhile, he had a sermon to write.

If the number of cars parked on the church lot was an indication, the social was a resounding success.

Maneuvering her midsize car into a minisize space, Matt set the hand brake and flashed a grin at her grandmother.

"Proud of yourself, are you?" Maddy Wolfe asked in a toast-dry tone of voice.

"It's in," Matt replied. "And without a scratch, or even a bump."

"Uh-huh. It's in," Maddy drawled. "Now the trick will be us...getting out."

"It was the last space, Gram."

"I know," Maddy agreed, releasing the seat belt.

A concerned line drawing her brows together, Matt glanced to the right, studying the narrow space between the car and the one parked next to it.

"I should have let you get out before I pulled in," she said in apology. "In fact, I suppose I should have let you off at the church entrance." There was no force on earth that would have made her admit that she had been distracted by the thought of seeing David Macdonough again.

Stupid…but there it was.

Maddy merely gave her a pained look. "Think I'm too old and decrepit to squeeze out of a cramped space or totter across a parking lot, do you?"

"No…I—" Matt began in protest, only to break off when she noticed the sparkle of laughter dancing in her grandmother's faded blue eyes. "Oh…you."

"Still rise to the bait," Maddy chided, carefully inching the door open so as not to bump the shiny new car next to Matt's. "Come Christmas, your cousins will have a field day teasing you."

"They'll try," Matt conceded, inching her own door open. "But I'll be prepared for them," she said pointedly, sinuously working her way out of the car. "I wasn't expecting it from you."

"I know." Maddy tossed her a smug look before exiting the vehicle with just a smidgen less agility than her granddaughter. "But, you see, I consider it my duty to keep you on your toes."

Laughing, Matt circled the car to the older woman's side. "You're a hoot, Gram," she said, linking her arm with Maddy's. "You know that?"

"I do my best, honey," Maddy said, her steps a far cry from tottering as they made for the side entrance to the building where a large sign read Social Room.

The room was spacious—and packed.

The spicy aroma of spaghetti sauce permeated the air and activated Matt's appetite.

"Smells good," she murmured, her mouth watering as she inhaled the distinctive scent.

"Yes, and they have a good turnout for it," Maddy said, patiently waiting behind a group crowding around the cloakroom.

"Excellent," Matt concurred, unobtrusively taking a protective stance behind the older woman. "I'm glad that snow Thursday evening was a fizzle. If it had continued, this affair might have been a washout."

"Maybe not," Maddy observed, glancing around her. "This appears to be a hardy bunch."

"Yeah." Matt's gaze tracked her grandmother's over the bright, expectant faces of the milling crowd. "They look hardy and hungry. I hope they've prepared enough spaghetti for the supper."

"You wouldn't be so worried about it, if you'd

eaten something for lunch,'' Maddy said, moving forward as the group in front of them dispersed.

After handing their coats to the teenage girl manning the cloakroom, they moved on to a young man stationed at the doorway, selling tickets for supper.

Standing in line again, Matt purchased two tickets. Then she and Maddy trailed the crowd, wending its way around the long tables set up to serve supper in the center of the large room.

Servers, mostly teenagers, were bustling about, placing utensils wrapped in paper napkins, small bowls of salad, and covered baskets of bread on the tables.

"From the looks of it," Maddy observed, indicating the youngsters, "we won't have long to wait."

"Mmm," Matt agreed, nodding, then slanting a grin at her grandmother at the low growling demand for sustenance from her stomach.

Maddy merely shook her head.

From the big room, they shuffled into a smaller adjacent room, where other tables were laid out with the crafts and baked goods on sale.

Content to follow wherever her grandmother chose to go, and growing hungrier by the minute, Matt surreptitiously skimmed the faces around her in the room. She was looking for one person in particular, a man even taller than herself.

Her perusal proved fruitless, and quashing an unacceptable sense of disappointment, Matt centered her attention on the hand-crafted Christmas tree ornament her grandmother was examining.

Maddy bought the ornament, then moved on to the next table, Matt playing the shadow in her wake.

"Those cookies look good," Maddy said at one of the tables, indicating a plastic-covered tray.

"Yes, they do," Matt agreed, but went on to qualify, "But I can't imagine any cookies tasting better than yours always do—and you've baked I don't know how many dozens these past couple of weeks."

"About twenty or so," Maddy said, chuckling. "But remember, in addition to your parents and sister, all your uncles, aunts and cousins will be at the house on Christmas. I know how quickly cookies can disappear when my sons and grandsons are around."

"Point taken," Matt conceded. She laughed, feeling a quickening anticipation for the visit from her family with the approaching holidays.

"Besides," Maddy went on, flicking a hand at the goodies under discussion. "I've never baked that kind, and they look delicious."

Obviously having overheard the conversation, the attractive blond woman behind the table offered one of the sweets to Maddy. "Try one," she invited, smiling. "The recipe's been in my family for generations—my great-great-grandmother brought it with her from Sweden."

Accepting the cookie, Maddy thanked the woman with a delighted smile.

While her grandmother enthusiastically consumed the sweet, Matt exchanged smiles with the other woman. She couldn't help noticing when her eyes suddenly lit up as if someone had turned on a switch behind them. She was wondering what had caused the bright animation when a velvet-cloaked, gravelly voice from behind her sent a thrill skipping up her spine.

"Well, Corine, as usual, you don't have to sell your baked goods, they sell themselves."

"Hi, Mac," the woman he'd called Corine responded, her voice breathy, her eyes even brighter than before. "How are things going in the kitchen?"

"The usual chaos." He laughed, and then his voice lowered to a rich, warm honey. "I'm glad you could make it today, Matt. Is this lovely lady your grandmother?"

The sound of her name on his lips affected Matt in a manner way out of proportion to the context of his remarks. She felt an immediate weakness, a searing warmth. So, of course, she steeled her spine and infused a chill reserve to overlay the inner heat.

"Hello, David," she said with cool composure she was light-years from feeling. "And, yes, this is my grandmother." Catching the gleam of sharp interest in Maddy's eyes, she went on. "Gram, this is the Reverend David Macdonough, the pastor of this church. David, my grandmother, Maddy Wolfe.''

A smile twitching the corners of his too attractive mouth, David extended his hand to the older woman. ''A pleasure, Mrs. Wolfe.''

''Maddy,'' she said, taking his hand in a grasp Matt knew to be surprisingly strong for a woman in her eighties. ''And the pleasure is mine, Reverend Macdonough.''

''Mac...please, Maddy,'' he returned, a startled burst of laughter erupting from his throat. ''And you have one impressive grip there, lady.''

''Why, thank you, Mac.'' Maddy beamed at him in an instantly besotted way that had Matt choking back a groan. ''Comes from handling a passel of strong sons and grandsons.'' She eyed Matt's imposing form, and grinned. ''Not to mention granddaughter.''

His blue eyes shimmering with amusement, David regarded Matt, running a glance the full six-foot length of her slender body. When his gaze returned to clash with hers, his eyes appeared to smolder with blue fire.

''Strong, are you?''

His eyes, his sexy voice, sent the heat tearing through her self-imposed chill reserve to slam into her with the force of a .44 slug. Stunned, Matt felt the heat radiating from within, singeing her cheeks.

Dammit. She hadn't blushed since she was fourteen. Desperate, she imposed an icy surface control.

"And hungry," she retorted, employing the steely tone she manufactured on the rare instances she had to deal with real hard cases. "Will you be serving supper anytime soon?"

"Matilda." The shocked-sounding murmur came from Maddy, who only ever used Matt's given name when she was out of patience with her.

In truth, Matt hadn't heard her Christian name from her grandmother for some years. At any other time, Matt would have heeded the exasperation in Maddy's voice. But not this time, not with this man.

Not even sure why she felt so threatened, so intimidated by the strength of his magnetic appeal, Matt narrowed her eyes and met his smoldering stare head-on.

David had the sheer masculine audacity to laugh in the face of her open defiance.

Matt's temper simmered.

"You'll have to excuse my granddaughter's rudeness, Mac," Maddy said, recognizing the signs of Matt's pending temper explosion. "She skipped lunch…" She paused to level a hard look on Matt. "I'm afraid she must be suffering a lack of nourishment to her mental capacity as well as her body."

"No offense taken, Maddy," David smoothly assured the older woman, sparing a gentle smile for her before returning his gaze to Matt.

Rebelliously refusing to back down, Matt arrogantly quirked a brow at him.

The corners of his lips twitched once more. "You're in luck, Matt," he said, laughter woven through his honeyed tones. "I came out of the kitchen for the express purpose of announcing that supper will be served in—" He broke off to glance at his watch. "In about ten or so minutes," he went on, motioning toward the larger room. "Why don't you escort your grandmother to a good table?"

"Thank you." Matt clipped the response. "I'll do that." She broke his unsettling eye contact to turn to her grandmother. "Ready, Gram?"

"In a minute," Maddy said, her eyes bright with speculation as she glanced from Matt to David. "I want to buy some of these cookies." She shifted another sharp-eyed look between the pair before turning to give her cookie order to the woman behind the table.

"That is one shrewd woman."

Matt started at the low, intimate sound of his voice close, too close, to her ear. Her heartbeat accelerated with the moist sensation of his warm breath feathering her skin. Her voice eluded her at the realization of how very close his mouth was to the curve of her jaw.

"Y-yes," Matt finally responded, damning the weak, fluttery sound of her own voice. The compelling urge to step aside, out of harm's way, both confused and annoyed her.

"And maybe even as strong as you."

Good grief. Matt stifled a protest. He had moved his head even closer to hers; his voice a mere whisper curling around her senses. Although he was not touching her, Matt could feel the heat from his body, smell the sheer male scent of him.

Excitement flared to life inside her...deep inside the most feminine part of her. She ached with a sudden and compelling need.

This is insane, she thought, gritting her teeth in an attempt to reassert control. Why on earth was she experiencing this wild, almost abandoned response to him? David's comments had been innocuous—but his voice, his tone...

"Forewarning, Matt Wolfe." The sound was little more than a breath. "I am stronger."

A challenge? Relief shivered through Matt—at least she assured herself the feeling was relief. She could deal with a challenge.

Drawing herself up to her full, squared-shouldered height, Matt stepped away, but only to allow herself room to turn and rake his admittedly impressive form with an unimpressed, sweeping glance.

"Indeed?" she drawled, her expression disdainful. "Don't bet the parsonage on it."

He laughed. "Oh, I think that would be a safe—"

"I'm ready now," Maddy said, unwittingly interrupting him. "Let's go find seats…before the stampede that's sure to follow Mac's announcement."

"Which I'd better get to," he said. He started to turn away, then slanted a sparkling look at Maddy. "May I join you ladies for supper?"

No. The refusal shouted inside Matt's head but her grandmother beat her by replying first.

"Why, we'd be delighted." She blessed him with a bright smile. "We'll save you a seat."

"Thank you," he responded, not sparing so much as a glance at Matt's set expression. "I'll only be a few minutes." Raising a hand, he smiled at the woman behind the table. "See you, Corine." Then he was gone.

"Yeah, see you."

The note of dejection in the other woman's voice snagged Matt's attention. Unaware of being observed, Corine's gaze was fastened on David's retreating back, a desolate, pained look in her eyes.

She's in love with him.

The realization caused conflicting emotions inside Matt. Because David had shown no signs of a reciprocal emotional involvement, she felt sympathy and compassion for the woman. She also felt something else, something unfamiliar.

While escorting her grandmother into the larger room, Matt mused in uncomfortable silence on the strange new sensation.

This feeling…surely it couldn't be jubilation? A

sense of extreme exhilaration because David apparently did not return Corine's affection?

Appalled at the very idea of feeling so much as a tinge of satisfaction in response to another's rejection, Matt dismissed the concept out of hand.

Even so…

"Why don't you sit over there?" Maddy's question broke through Matt's unpalatable introspection. "I'll sit here and save this seat for Mac."

Collecting herself, Matt took the end seat at the long table. She frowned at the empty chair opposite her, on which Maddy deposited her purse and bag of cookies.

"This table doesn't suit you?" Maddy asked, obviously noting Matt's expression.

"The table?" Matt's frown darkened. Then, realizing she was causing her grandmother concern, she dredged up a smile. "It's fine, Gram. I'm sorry, I was…um, distracted."

"Is something wrong?" Maddy raised her eyebrows.

"No, no, I…"

"May I have your attention, please?" The sound of David's voice, deep and exciting even over the PA system, saved Matt from her sense of ineptitude.

"Supper will be served in approximately five minutes. It's open seating in the social room. Please place your meal ticket on the table. Thank you, and we hope you enjoy your meal."

Matt dug in her pocket for the tickets she had purchased and placed them on the table.

"Mac is one very attractive man," Maddy said, almost too casually. "Isn't he?"

"I suppose." Matt managed an equally casual tone, and a disinterested shrug. To underline her lack of concern for the subject, she speared a wedge of tomato from her salad bowl and popped it into her mouth.

"The devil dances in his eyes."

Matt started, nearly choking on the partially chewed tomato.

"Gram, really. The man is an ordained minister of the church," she protested, even though she herself had noted the devilish light in his eyes.

Maddy gave her a wry look. "I don't want to shatter any preconceptions, dear, but ordained ministers who have not taken a vow of celibacy are as subject to human frailties as the rest of us," she said with gentle humor. "Or have you forgotten that our own church pastor has three children and five grandchildren?"

Matt gave an impatient shake of her head, and gulped down the mangled tomato wedge before attempting to answer. "No, of course not, but..."

"Why don't you go get us some water?" Maddy inserted into Matt's sputter. She waved at a small table along the wall on which pitchers of iced water and stacks of brightly colored plastic cups were set. "I think you need a drink."

Grateful for the reprieve, however short-lived, Matt jumped up and went for the water.

Her smile serene, innocent, Maddy waited until Matt had returned with the drinks and had taken a sip of the cool water, before broadsiding her with another question.

"You're having trouble with the concept of our pastor as a sexual being?"

Matt was glad she had swallowed the water, for she surely would have sprayed the table with her jolt of surprise at her grandmother's phrasing. And, the thing of it was, Maddy seemed so comfortable with the topic.

"Well, no," Matt said, striving to appear as blasé as her grandmother. "But..."

"What?" Maddy grinned.

"I don't know." Matt was floundering, badly, and she knew it. Why she was floundering, she was afraid to delve into. "I just can't imagine anyone ever having given a thought to our pastor in that way...or noting the devil dancing in his eyes."

"But then, you didn't know the man when he was young," Maddy noted pointedly. "I did."

"You're kidding?" Matt exclaimed, surprised and amused by the very idea of the gentle, timid pastor she knew revealed in this new light.

"No," Maddy said complacently. "He was quite

the dapper fellow...when he was young. But, mind you, he was always a fine man and pastor.''

"I don't doubt it," Matt said, fascinated by the dreamy look on Maddy's face.

A smile, youthful, wholly feminine, curved her lips. "I must admit, though, that he was never as fine a figure of a man, or nearly as good-looking, as Mac.''

Matt simply stared at her grandmother's rapt expression, then her attention was caught by two doors being swung open at the far end of the room. A line of servers, ranging from early teens to middle age, each bearing large serving trays, exited the kitchen. Her stomach gave a rumble of appreciation.

She shifted her gaze back to her grandmother, to inform her that supper was being served. Her words were lost to the speculative look on Maddy's face.

"Yes, Mac is one good-looking, tough-looking, sexy-looking man," Maddy reiterated—with a flourish.

Matt had to laugh, despite herself. "Why, Gram. Darned if you don't sound smitten with the man."

"In a certain way, I guess I am," Maddy said enigmatically, her eyes fairly dancing with some inner delight. "But, more importantly, are you?"

"Me? I?" Matt blurted. Oh, hell, she thought, suddenly feeling cornered.

Smitten with the man...with David?

Ridiculous.

"Gram, really," she said, trying—and failing—for a note of repression. She was reaching, and the only defense she could grab hold of was a factor her consciousness had secretly acknowledged from the beginning.

"The man has got to be ten, possibly…probably, more than ten years older than I am."

"Indeed?" Maddy's smile was unruffled. "What a coincidence. Your grandfather was twelve years older than I am. And I took one look at him and knew."

Knew? Knew? At that moment, the only thing Matt knew was that she felt disoriented, confused, leagues out of her depth. No, she corrected herself. That wasn't quite all she knew. She knew, as well, that there was a magnetic quality about David Macdonough that drew her in some inexplicable, irrevocable way.

The very thought of an inevitable attraction was unnerving, almost frightening. Seemingly without effort, he generated an excitement inside her unlike anything she had ever before experienced.

But what was even more unnerving to Matt, was her apparent transparency. If her grandmother saw her unwilling response to him, did David see it, too?

Stunned by the idea and the ramifications it implied, Matt maintained her grandmother's bright gaze for some seconds. When she glanced away it was only to have her breath stolen. For her vision was filled with the sight of the very man they were speaking of striding along...and heading directly toward her.

Matt had a compelling impulse to bolt.

Chapter 5

Maintaining her seat, and her fragile grasp on her composure, Matt managed a strained smile. She murmured "Thank you" to the thirty-something-year-old man who deposited three heaping plates of steaming, aromatic pasta onto the table.

David waited until the man had finished serving the others seated at the long table. Then the handsome pastor slid into his seat opposite Matt.

"So, how was the salad, ladies?" He raised his dark brows and shared a smile between Matt and Maddy.

"I enjoyed mine," Maddy replied in a rather wry voice that matched her smile. "I don't know about Matt...since she barely touched hers."

He glanced at the bowl in question, then fixed a probing look on Matt. "It's not to your taste?"

"It's fine," she said, shooting a reproachful look at her grandmother.

"But then—" he began.

"I didn't want to take the edge off of my appetite," she cut in, her tone sharp. "Okay?" she demanded, wincing as her companions responded in unison.

"Matt!" Maddy reprimanded.

"Sure." David shrugged.

Matt felt both chastised and childish. She didn't particularly like the feelings. So, of course, she lay the blame on him…to herself, at any rate. She wasn't about to incur more disfavor with her grandmother by voicing her thoughts out loud.

"Sorry, but I am hungry." She made the half-hearted apology, and followed it with a muttered request. "Does anyone mind if I eat…before it gets cold?"

Maddy shook her head in despair of her granddaughter's display of bad manners.

"Dig in," David invited, his lips curving in a blatant and thoroughly sexy male grin.

The strange sensation that coiled through Matt's stomach had nothing whatsoever to do with the tantalizing smell of the spaghetti.

Darn his attractive hide. What did he think he was doing? Matt railed in silent frustration while making a performance of coolly twirling the saucy pasta onto her fork. *He was a minister, for goodness' sake.*

Matt raised her eyes to his as she slipped the fork into her mouth. An electrifying jolt sizzled through her from the heat in his eyes, which were fastened on her lips.

Oh, mercy, she thought, shivering in response to the fiery gaze searing her mouth.

"Good?" David's voice held pure innocence while his eyes conveyed the exact opposite.

Matt felt another jolt zip through her, leaving her weak, quivering, aching for...

Chill out, Wolfe, Matt told herself in exasperation. Tearing her gaze from his, she quickly tried to repair the breach in her defenses. With intense concentration, she chewed the pasta and swallowed.

"So?"

Matt glanced up, frowning at the prompting tone in his voice. "So what?"

David blessed her with a gentle, infuriatingly tolerant smile. "Do you like it?"

Distracted by his annoying smile, Matt missed the point of his question. "Like what?"

Maddy made a snorting sound and rolled her eyes.

"The spaghetti, Officer Matt," David said in obvious amusement. "What else?"

Lord help her, for it was apparent she was too addle-brained to help herself, Matt reflected miserably. What had she done? What grievous sin had she committed to be condemned to the punishment of this overwhelming attraction to David Macdonough?

Maddy sighed into the lengthening silence. "The spaghetti is delicious, Mac," she said, a tinge of youthful impishness in her smile. "The sauce is almost as good as my own."

"High praise, indeed, I'm sure." David flashed his pearly whites at Maddy, but quickly returned his drilling gaze back to her granddaughter. "Do you agree, Matt?"

She blinked, feeling dumber by the second. "About it being high praise? Yes, of course."

"No, Matt, not about the praise," he said kindly, as if he were addressing a sweet but rather dull child. "I meant, do you agree that the meal is delicious?"

Good night nurse, Matt groused to herself. Why was he so blasted intent on getting her opinion, anyway? Feeling badgered, she heaved a sigh.

"Yes, David, I do agree," she replied, her tone one of long-suffering exasperation. "The meal is delicious. I'd love to be allowed to savor it in peace."

Maddy arched a brow in warning.

To Matt's chagrin, the aggravating man had the gall to grin at her.

"Glad you like it," he drawled, as if, after all his probing efforts, it was of little matter or concern to him.

On the very edge of exploding, Matt gritted her teeth and turned her attention to her supper.

Fortunately, for her peace of already rattled mind, David followed her example. The remainder of the meal was consumed in nerve-settling quiet.

In truth, Matt did agree that the spaghetti was delicious. She cleaned her plate of every piece of long, thin pasta and every morsel of meatball. Stuffed and contented, she placed her fork on her plate, convinced she could not eat another bite.

However, no sooner had she sat back in her chair when the troop of servers returned. Working like a well-rehearsed unit, one group whipped the plates from the table, only to be followed by another group, some serving smaller plates containing individually wrapped slices of Neapolitan ice cream, others steaming cups of coffee and tiny cups of half-and-half.

Although her table companions appeared to welcome both, Matt accepted the coffee but passed on the ice cream with a murmured, "No thanks."

Carefully sipping the hot, full-bodied brew, Matt studied her grandmother, noting the telltale signs of weariness about her eyes and mouth.

Time to go home, she thought, reminding herself—as she often had to do—of her grandmother's age. In light of Maddy's robust health and sharp mental activity, her advanced years were easy to forget.

The woman was obviously beginning to tire and, ever protective of her beloved grandmother, Matt suggested leaving as soon as Maddy finished her dessert and coffee.

"I've got a few things to do yet tonight," she tacked on, so that her grandmother wouldn't think she was being too overprotective.

"Yes, I'm ready," Maddy said, her smile a clear indication that she was on to Matt's ploy. She pushed her chair back just as a middle-aged couple came to a stop next to Mac.

"Well, you certainly haven't lost your touch, Mac," the man said, grasping the pastor's extended hand. "Your spaghetti sauce was excellent...as always."

"Yes, it was wonderful, Mac," the woman chimed in. "I wish I could cook it as good as you."

More than a little surprised, Matt stared in bemusement as, with a flashing smile, David stood to thank the couple and exchange a few pleasantries.

"You cooked the spaghetti sauce?" Matt blurted out without thinking when the couple moved on.

"Yes." Not a hint of either false modesty or overt pride shaded his tone. He shrugged. "But I had a lot of help from our active parishioners."

"Nevertheless, you make a mean sauce, Mac," Maddy said, standing and offering her hand to him. "And it's been a pleasure meeting you."

"The pleasure was mine." David returned the compliment. "I'm glad you came." He sifted a gleaming glance at Matt. "You, too," he added softly.

"I enjoyed it," Matt lied, suddenly feeling pressured, her breathing constrained. Standing, she faced him—not quite eye to eye. Her eyes were more at the level of his chin. She didn't like the four or so inches in height he had over her. She didn't offer her hand, either.

"You know," he said just as Matt made to turn away. "I give a pretty mean sermon, too. I'd be pleased to have the both of you attend services some Sunday."

Not in this lifetime, Matt thought, and opened her mouth to tell him so. But her grandmother beat her to it.

"We just might take you up on that invitation," Maddy said, beaming at him.

David beamed back at her. Then gave a sidelong look at Matt. "I'll be looking forward to seeing you there someday."

Managing a weak smile and a mumbled response, Matt hustled her frowning grandmother away to collect their coats.

To her despair, David dogged their retreat, chatting with Maddy. His eyes laughing at Matt every foot of the way out.

Matt's constrained breathing didn't regulate until farewells had finally been exchanged and the door to the social room closed behind her—with David on the other side.

"What a charming man," Maddy said, her steps not as brisk on the return trip to the car.

"Yeah. Charming," Matt agreed through teeth gritted in baffling frustration.

"What's the matter with you?" Maddy demanded. "You've been acting strange all evening." She eyed Matt with obvious concern. "Are you coming down with a cold or something?"

On the verge of saying no, that she was feeling fine, Matt caught herself in time to grab at the excuse for her unusual behavior.

"I, uh, don't know. Maybe. I am feeling a little tired and washed out."

"Mmm," Maddy murmured, her sharp-eyed gaze skeptical. "Then I don't suppose you'll feel like accepting Mac's invitation to services tomorrow. Will you?"

Matt was once again on the verge of saying no when the realization struck her of her intended purpose for attending the church supper. She had planned to cast a professional eye over David's parishioners...and the only person there that she had really seen was David.

And there hadn't been one damn professional thing about her regard.

"Well?" Maddy's prodding voice held an edge of impatience at Matt's lengthy silence.

Matt sighed. She was a cop—with a job to do. She could not, would not, allow her personal feelings to interfere.

She didn't want to see David again. He unnerved her, made her experience confusing and conflicting emotions. In truth, he scared the hell out of her.

But...

"I don't know," she finally said, shrugging. "Let's wait until morning, see how I feel."

It was very late, and Mac was very much awake...awake and aching. He hadn't even attempted to court sleep. The bed was the absolute last place he wanted to be. It conjured thoughts both beguiling and bedeviling.

Standing at the bedroom window, Mac stared up into the clear, star-bright sky.

Is this a test, Sir? Mac asked his Maker in his less than traditional manner of praying. Military trained, he thought it the highest form of address for his ultimate Commander.

In Your infinite wisdom, have You visited this mental and physical affliction upon me to gauge the depth of my devotion, faith and commitment?

But no... In Your infinite wisdom, You know the depth of my commitment to Your service.

Still, there is this woman, this tall cop who turns me on something fierce.

What to do about it...and her.

I know, I know… You endowed mankind with intelligence and free will…the ability to reason through our little problems, and hopefully arrive at a rational and workable resolution.

On the other hand, You also endowed mankind with sensuality, and the powerful urge to procreate, which necessitates the coming together of a male and a female in the sexual act.

That inner drive within me, so long dormant, has reasserted itself, and is now running hot and strong in my system.

Is it wrong, Sir, to desire the company and communion of another?

What to do? How to proceed?

Sighing, Mac blinked, bringing the diamond-bright sky back into focus. His expression contemplative, he turned away from the window, then paused. He frowned for a moment before swinging back around. A faint smile feathered his lips as he tilted his head to gaze once again up into the clear night sky.

The full meaning of the contents of his silent prayer echoed inside his mind.

Mankind was endowed with sensuality and the powerful urge to procreate.

Of course, he thought, wondering, as he had many times before, at the endless intelligence and love of the Supreme Being.

Thank you, Sir, for your bottomless wisdom.

Pivoting away from the window, Mac began to undress for bed, his conscience no longer troubled. Savoring his renewed sexual vigor, he crawled between the cool sheets, his course set in his mind.

He had plans for Miss Matilda Wolfe, plans both sensual and honorable…as the Good Lord certainly knew.

Mac slept the peaceful sleep of the innocent.

Dressed in a white silk shirt and a chocolate brown suit that nearly matched the color of her eyes, Matt strode into the kitchen Sunday morning. Her grandmother was seated at the table, a half slice of toast in her hand, a cup of coffee in front of her.

"Morning, Gram," Matt said, glancing at the clock and deciding she had time for a cup of the aromatic brew before they had to go. "I'll be ready to leave for church whenever you are."

"But…" Maddy frowned. "Have you forgotten?"

Her coffee poured, Matt crossed to the table and sat opposite her grandmother. "Forgotten?" Now she frowned. "Forgotten what?"

Maddy sighed—as mothers and grandmothers had sighed over the young since day one. "Matt, I told you last Monday that the Bakers would be picking me up for church this morning."

"Oh, yes." Her memory jogged, Matt did remember. "You said that after services you and the Bakers

would be stopping somewhere for lunch before going to the nursing home to visit Mrs. Baker's sister.''

"That's right," Maddy said, her smile one of patient acceptance of youth. "I also said we would
probably stop for supper on the way home, if you'll
recall. You assured me you could muddle through
on your own."

"And I can." Matt could also understand how the
information had slipped her mind. She had been
rather distracted since the night of the incident at
David's church. "You've trained me very well in
that respect," she went on in a teasing tone.

Smiling, Maddy lifted her cup to take a sip of the
coffee, a speculative gleam in her eyes. "Are you
still going to church?" she asked.

"Might as well." Matt shrugged. "I'm up and
dressed for it."

"You know…" Maddy murmured, an almost too
casual inflection in her voice. "This might be a good
time for you to take Mac up on his invitation and
attend services at his church instead of ours."

A thrill streaked down Matt's spine, part trepidation, part anticipation, and wholly excitement. The
inner conflict kept her mute for a moment, sifting
the pros and cons in her mind. The cons weighed
heavily.

"Oh, Gram, I don't know…" Her voice trailed
away as she realized the merit of her grandmother's
suggestion. Attending services at David's church

would offer her the opportunity to perform the duty she had failed to complete last night—that of running a professional glance over the members of David's parishioners.

Of course, it would also give her opportunity of seeing and talking to—sparring with?—David again.

The pros gained the upper hand.

"Then again, perhaps you're right," she murmured, hiding behind the cup she'd raised to her lips.

"Of course, I'm right."

Matt shot a glance at her. Was she imagining things, or had there been a thread of satisfaction woven through her grandmother's placid tones?

Maddy avoided Matt's probing look by turning to peer at the clock.

"Oh, my, will you look at the time," she said, standing and carrying her cup and plate to the sink. "I've got to get a move on, or I won't be ready when the Bakers arrive to collect me."

Could her grandmother be playing matchmaker? Matt mused. Suspicion aroused, she watched the elderly woman flutter about, rinsing her dishes, stashing them in the sink, and averting Matt's contemplative gaze as she hurried from the kitchen.

Brooding, Matt absently drank her coffee. She had to be mistaken. Maddy had never before presumed to nudge Matt in the direction of a man, any man.

On the other hand, Matt mused, she couldn't recollect her grandmother ever fluttering before, either.

"The Bakers are here, and I'm off, Matt," the woman in question called from the living room. "Have a nice day, and be sure you have something substantial for dinner this evening."

"Okay, I—" Matt broke off at the sound of the closing door... Why bother to continue, she'd only be talking to herself.

The church parking lot was nearly as full of cars as it had been the previous night. It would appear, Matt mused as she wedged her car between a sports coup and a van, that David could draw a crowd.

After being swept along by a buffeting cold wind, she was glad to get inside the church where it was warm. It was also full. Skimming the interior, Matt noticed a space at the end of a row a little to the back of the room's center.

Perfect for her purposes, she thought, removing her coat as she strode down the center aisle, then slipped onto the hard wooden pew.

"Good morning," said the middle-aged gentleman seated in the pew a foot or so from her.

"Good morning," Matt returned, her greeting smile quickly turning to a frown. "I hope I haven't taken a place you were holding for someone."

"No." He gave a reassuring shake of his head. "The seat was up for grabs."

Smiling, she folded her coat into the space separating them.

The man offered her a hymnal, and the page number of the first hymn to be sung.

With a murmured, "Thank you," Matt searched out the correct page.

A moment later the service began.

The hymn was sung.

Then David was there at the pulpit—no, not David, but the Reverend Macdonough. He looked solemn, imposing and a bit intimidating. In his clerical robes, he appeared larger, taller than memory served.

He began the service.

Matt didn't hear a word of it for the sound of her thumping heart pounding against her eardrums. All she heard was the honeyed-gravel sound of his voice, stroking her senses, abrading her nerves.

She felt chilled, and then hot. She couldn't take her eyes off of him.

In minute detail Matt studied the stern set of his strong, rough-hewn features, the slight arch of his dark brows, the thrust of his squared jawline, the sensuous definition of his masculine mouth.

Longing, deep and primal, swept through her, firing her blood, and imagination.

She ached something awful.

Someone behind her coughed.

Reason reasserted itself.

Appalled by the intensity of her reaction, she reminded herself of where she was, and why she was supposedly there. Matt tore her rapt gaze from his alluring figure and applied herself to the congregation.

Trying to appear casual, she glanced around, and was immediately struck by the expressions on the faces she could see. Every one of them, young and old, appeared enthralled, either by the pastor's voice, or the content of his message.

Matt didn't see so much as a shading hint of guilt or furtiveness on any face. If the perpetrator of the desecration was there, he or she either felt no guilt or remorse, or had carefully hidden it.

Her questing gaze skimmed over, paused, then zapped back to hone in on a woman seated two rows farther back and to the other side of the aisle. The woman appeared to be in her mid-thirties...and not at all well. Her face, once attractive, Matt was certain, was pale and drawn, and she looked exhausted.

She had two children with her, a boy about eighteen months or so, who she held on her lap, and a pretty girl about eleven years old.

Matt felt a pang of compassion when the woman quickly raised a hand to muffle a cough, causing the girl to glance at her in anxious concern.

The woman smiled and murmured something to the girl that eased the strain on the child's face.

Matt's gaze moved on.

When the service was over, and the final hymn sung, Matt moved with the crowd heading for the door…and the robed man exchanging greetings as they exited.

When she drew even with him, Matt accepted his extended hand. She had no other choice but to do so. But at least he was David again.

"Glad you could make it, Matt." David's hand was warm and strong around hers. He raised a brow. "But where is your grandmother?"

"She had a previous commitment," she explained, taking a step to move on. He kept her in place by tightening his grasp on her hand.

"I'd appreciate it if you'd hang around until I'm through here." Though soft, his voice held more command than request. "I'd like a word with you, hear the results of your observations."

She hesitated, wanting to stay yet somehow knowing that she shouldn't.

"I'll give you lunch."

Matt was beginning to feel embarrassed. Didn't the man care that he had an audience?

"Will you wait?" he persisted, giving evidence of his unconcern…or his knowledge of the regard in which he was held by his parishioners.

Matt caved.

"Yes, I'll wait."

Chapter 6

Not wanting to draw attention, and speculation, to herself, Matt didn't drive from the lot to his house. She waited in her car.

Five, ten, fifteen minutes she waited. It would appear his parishioners were a chatty bunch.

And all the time she waited, Matt chastised herself for agreeing to speak with him in private. Since she hadn't noticed anything out of the ordinary about any one member of his congregation, she had made no observations worth mentioning to him.

And she certainly hadn't agreed to wait because he had promised her lunch; she could get lunch anywhere. Besides, she wasn't even hungry. She was too churned up inside, too edgy, too...

Not wanting to go where her thoughts were leading, Matt directed her attention to the cars exiting the parking lot in slow progression.

Finally, a woman hurried to the last remaining car. It was Corine, the woman David had introduced to Matt the night before, the one whose sad-eyed gaze had followed him when he had walked away.

Matt couldn't help but notice the quick look Corine shot at her car, or the expression of frustrated envy marring her pretty face.

Telling herself she needed another woman's antipathy like she needed a bout of the flu, Matt reached for the ignition key.

At that moment, David exited a side entrance of the church, his long-legged stride bringing him to her car in seconds. Opening the passenger door, he slid onto the seat beside Matt.

"Ready for lunch?"

Matt wanted to say no. And she would have, if his smile, his voice, hadn't been so...so friendly.

She caved again. "I suppose."

He indicated the turnoff driveway to his house. "Then, lead on MacWolf."

Failing to control the twitch of amusement on her lips, Matt rolled her eyes and set the car in motion.

"Is there something I can do to help?" Matt felt awkward and uncomfortable just standing in the center of David's kitchen.

Busy gathering ingredients to prepare their lunch, he slanted a quick smile at her over his shoulder.

"No, I've got everything under control." His hands and arms full of food, he backed away from the fridge and shut the door with his hip. "Have a seat. Coffee will be ready in a few minutes."

"But…" she started to protest.

He wasn't listening. "While I cook, you can fill me in on the observations you made in church."

Sighing, Matt slid into a chair. "What I observed was a group of normal, well-mannered, and very attentive, respectful people. I didn't spot one individual who appeared either disgruntled or guilty-looking."

The utter conviction in her voice brought him around to smile at her. His relief was obvious.

"That's a load off my mind." His smile faded. "But, that puts us right back at square one."

"'Fraid so." She nodded.

"I feel I must warn you that, if this was a random act of vandalism, we may never find the perpetrator."

He lifted his rather spectacular shoulders in a slight, hopeless-looking shrug.

"I know that—I knew it all along. I just thought it was worth your time to have a look at my congregation."

"It was," she agreed.

Nodding, he turned to the business of preparing

lunch. His softened voice drifted to her. "I also thought it was an excellent excuse to see you again."

Matt didn't respond; she couldn't. She was too busy dealing with the tingling sensations his bald statement sent skittering through her.

This did not bode well, she warned herself. But her greedy gaze continued feasting on his tall, leanly muscled form.

Damn. No man should look that good in faded jeans and an old sweatshirt...most especially not a man of the cloth, she reflected.

"Are you sure there isn't something I can do to help?" she asked, feeling the need for a distraction from her own thoughts, and her hungry gaze.

"No." He turned from the sink to flash an unrepentant grin at her. "I'm afraid that I'm one of those infamous temperamental cooks who won't tolerate anyone else at the stove with me."

Matt returned his grin with a wry smile.

"But," he qualified, chuckling, "I have no objections to you setting the table."

"Okay...I can handle that." Matt got up from the chair. But before she took a step he halted her with his upraised hand.

"Not yet. I'll tell you when."

She lifted one eyebrow. "And what am I supposed to do in the meantime?"

His grin flashed again. "Make yourself at home. You can hang your coat there in the closet by the back door." He gave a flick of one hand. "And there's a powder room off the hallway there..." He flicked his hand in the opposite direction. "In case you want to freshen up...or something."

Matt stood there a moment, feeling useless. When he turned back to the sink, she heaved a sigh and carried her coat to the closet.

She wandered through the kitchen and into the hallway. After washing her hands in the powder room, she ambled into the living room.

As she had noticed when she had been there before, the home's furnishings, while tasteful and of excellent quality, were spare. In the case of an area in front of the picture window, completely bare. Matt wondered if the lack of decorative touches was because of his being fairly new to the house or simply because of his bachelorhood.

She ambled into the dining room which was also sparsely furnished. But there was a large oak table set in the center of the room, the top nearly concealed by boxes of assorted sizes. Upon investigation, she was pleased to find the boxes contained a glittering array of Christmas decorations. This explained that bare spot in the living room. Obviously, David was planning to set his tree in front of the window.

"Coffee's ready, Matt," David called from the kitchen. "You can set the table now. Lunch is just about done."

And none too soon, she thought, her mouth watering at the aroma that greeted her when she entered the kitchen.

Since collecting the plates, utensils and such necessitated skirting around him, Matt knew at once she should have kept her mouth shut about wanting to help in some way. Other than to cease breathing, there was no way for her to avoid inhaling the distinctive scent of him—the combined smells of spicy soap, spicy aftershave, and even spicier pure male.

Heady stuff, for sure.

By the time David was ready to serve their lunch, Matt felt positive she could not manage to eat a thing.

"Where did you learn to cook like this?" Matt asked. She was savoring the last bite of the delicious, featherlight Western omelet which—despite her fears to the contrary—she'd devoured like a starving person.

"It's a long story," David said, rising to retrieve the coffeepot and refill their cups. "And not a particularly pretty one, at that."

"I have all day." Matt found her reply shocking. Yet she was intrigued despite her reservations about spending more time in his disturbing company.

"I was in the military—" he began.

"You were a cook in the army?" she interrupted in a burst of surprise. "Weren't you a chaplain?"

"No, Matt." His smile was wry. "I was in the Special Services."

"Oh." Matt frowned at the effort of making a connection between the Special Services and the ministry.

"I know it's a reach," he said, grinning. "But there is a bridge between the two."

Did she really want to cross that bridge? Matt asked herself. She was curious—who wouldn't be? Even so, curiosity aside, did she really want to know his history, considering the effect he had on her? If she had an ounce of self-preservation, she mused, she'd stop him now, make her excuses and run like...

Too late, David led her onto that bridge.

His voice devoid of inflection, his words concise, he gave her a brief account of his service time, his special assignments. It was all very exciting, but not unexpected in light of his military status.

But then Matt felt her nerves quiver with apprehension when tension tightened his features, and his voice.

"My personal turning point came near the end of my second tour of duty." He paused to offer her a faint smile.

"I had planned to re-up, again." He shrugged, the movement looked anything but casual.

"We were assigned to Africa, to yet another emerging country torn by warring factions. Our mission was to distribute food—not interference, just bring food to the starving people who had fled their homes to escape the carnage.'' He closed his eyes a moment, as if marshaling his thoughts—and courage.

Without conscious direction, Matt reached across the table and grasped his hand. "It erupted in your faces." It was an easy deduction; it had happened before, many times before.

"Yeah." He exhaled. "The one faction hit us. I didn't even know which side, the current rulers or the supposed freedom fighters. They were all over us like a swarm of angry bees.'' He shook his head and gave a cynical laugh. "It was sheer pandemonium. We were ordered to pull back.'' His voice rang hollow; his eyes looked haunted. "That's when I saw him."

"'Him'?" Matt repeated, thinking he surely thought he had seen a vision of the Lord.

"The child," he said. "A boy, around five or six. He was nothing but skin and bones, and he was injured and bleeding from a bullet wound in his side. And his eyes... Oh, God, his eyes."

He fell silent. His own eyes, now the darkest blue, stared into the distance—or the past.

Matt was silent, too. What could she possibly say? She tightened her hand around his. David blinked, and shuddered.

"He was lying by the side of the dirt road, staring

at me. He didn't cry out in pain, or call to me for help. But then, he didn't need to say a word. His eyes were eloquent.''

''You couldn't leave him behind.'' This guess was even easier than the first.

''No, despite orders of no physical involvement, I could not leave him behind,'' he said.

''What did you do?'' she asked, aware of the penalties for disobeying orders.

''I scooped him up into my arms and ran like hell.'' His voice grew strained, and picked up speed.

''My unit had faded into the cover of the surrounding bush. I could hear my buddy yelling at me, urging me on. I had almost made it to the brush when I was hit.'' His body jerked, as if he'd actually felt the shot.

''You were captured?''

''No.'' David shook his head. ''I barely felt it:...then. I kept running, crashing into the brush, and straight into my buddy's arms.'' Pain, deep, emotional pain, flickered over his taut face. ''It was all for nothing. I wasn't fast enough.'' His voice was raw. ''The boy was dead.''

The heavy weight of silence settled in the room, and into Matt's shocked mind. For long moments she couldn't think, react. Numb, she stared at him.

The crushing grip of his hand brought her back to reality. Matt half expected to hear her knuckles pop in response to his hard clasp on her fingers. Pain streaked up her arm; she clamped her lips against a cry of distress, wondering at the power of the protective surge she felt for him.

"David," she said calmly, softly.

His body jolted as if she had shouted at him. Then his eyes came into focus. "What?"

"You're..." Matt managed a strained smile. "You're hurting my hand."

"Good God." His fingers sprang apart, releasing her.

"Matt, I'm sorry...I—"

"No." She cut him off, shaking her head. "It's all right. I understand."

"It's not all right." Scowling, he gently cradled her abused hand in his palm. "Please, forgive me, Matt. I...er, wasn't really here." Then, slowly lifting her hand, he brought her palm to his lips.

A different sensation, the complete opposite of pain, streaked up Matt's arm. It shimmered like a sun-spangled waterfall through her body.

Matt caught back the gasp that rose to her throat, and from somewhere found the sense to distract him.

"And you...your wound?" Her eyes made a quick appraisal of his solid form. She'd never before noticed any apparent effects inflicted by the bullet. At least, there were no physical aftereffects.

A self-deprecating smile shadowed his terse mouth.

"I was flown back to the States, to a military hospital. The physical wound healed." He went on, as if his thoughts had monitored hers. "But the mental damage was devastating—it damn near destroyed me."

That was the second time she had heard him swear in the retelling, which told her a lot about what he'd been through. Matt bit her lip until it hurt. She was almost afraid to ask, and yet, for reasons she had no desire to delve into, she had to know.

"How...how did you overcome the mental anguish?"

David laughed. It was not a pleasant sound. "For a long time, I didn't overcome it. I didn't even try."

"Your family?" Matt murmured.

"All gone." He winced. "But that's another story. After losing my mother, then my father—" he sighed "—and then my younger sister, the military, the discipline, kept me from going off the rails."

When he paused, Matt shivered, for his eyes had taken on that dark blue, distant expression once more.

"But after that debacle, the military became the cause, not the cure." His tones were as dark as his eyes. "That boy's big, pleading eyes tormented me, wouldn't let me rest."

"Oh, David," she murmured.

He moved his shoulders, figuratively shaking off her sympathetic concern. A self-derisive smile curled his tight lips.

"By the time my wound had healed, my tour of duty was out. I didn't reenlist. Instead, I plunged into self-pity. It was an easy move from there into alcohol, and from there into degradation." Disgust colored his voice. "I wallowed in it…booze, women, panhandling, outright begging. You name it, I probably indulged in it."

Disbelief widened Matt's eyes. This man? This pastor who had earned the obvious respect and devotion of his congregation? He was so gentle, so good. No. No. She could not, would not, accept it.

Matt wasn't even aware that she slowly moved her head in mute denial.

"Yes, Matt. It's true…all of it."

"Drugs, too?" Matt nearly choked on the words.

"Surprisingly…no." He gave a humorless chuckle. "Even in the deepest depths of despair, something inside me resisted that form of self-destruction."

"But looking at you now…" Confusion clouded her thoughts and speech. "How…"

"How did I make it from there to here?" A hopeful strand of genuine amusement enriched his velvet-coated, gravelly voice.

"Yes… I mean…" She shrugged.

"I know what you mean." He pushed away from the table and stood. "And I'll explain…after I get something to drink. All that talking has me parched."

"And me," she said, wetting her dry lips. It wasn't until the tension suddenly drained from her that Matt realized that throughout his recitation she had been wound up as tight as a spool of thread.

He smiled in understanding. "More coffee? Iced tea? Cola?"

"Something cold," she decided aloud. "Iced tea sounds wonderful."

"Coming up." Turning, David went to a cabinet and withdrew an automatic iced-tea machine, then set about brewing their drinks.

While he busied himself with the tea, Matt cleared the table of their forgotten plates, cups and utensils. She was wiping the table when he announced that the tea was ready.

Once again seated opposite each other at the table, tall ice-filled glasses in front of them, David launched back into his story.

"You wondered how I got from my self-created hell to here," he began.

A sip of tea in her mouth, Matt nodded.

He smiled in remembrance. "A very down-to-earth, very tough angel yanked me out of it."

Angel? Matt frowned.

David laughed. "Really." A flickering shadow banished his laughter. "She's gone now...hopefully to a justly earned reward. I received word of her demise a month or so before I was assigned here to Sprucewood." He slowly shook his head. "I hadn't even known she was ill, or I'd have gone to her...given my own life for her, if I could.'' He sighed. ''She knew that, of course, which was why she didn't let me know, I'm sure.''

''But...who was she?'' Matt asked, for some reason expecting to be given the name of a sister of mercy or a missionary.

''Her name was Rachel Rosenberg.''

''She was Jewish!'' Matt exclaimed without thinking.

''She was Jewish.'' His humor was back, tugging his lips into a soft smile. ''She was in her sixties, short, more than a little overweight—'' his eyes glowed with the light of pure love ''—and the most beautiful person it has ever been my privilege to know.''

An emotional lump lodged in Matt's throat. ''Tell me about her...please.''

He was quiet a moment, his expression contemplative. ''How to describe Rachel,'' he began, his voice touched with aching gentleness. He smiled. ''She loved the human race, no matter what color, creed, religious belief or station in life. To me, Rachel was the living, breathing embodiment of a handmaiden of the Lord. She was a very soft touch—and a very hard cookie.'' He chuckled. ''She lived, defined, the expression of tough love.''

''Sounds formidable,'' Matt murmured.

The sudden sparkle in David's eyes stole her breath—and melted her heart.

"You don't know the half of it. She was a veritable warrior in the service of saving supposed lost souls," he said, once again shaking his head, almost as if even he couldn't believe it. "I had been on the skids for about a year when she hauled me out of the gutter."

Matt gave a startled gasp.

He grinned. "Well, not precisely the gutter," he qualified. "Actually, I was curled up in a rat-infested, filthy alleyway—which didn't matter, because I was every bit as filthy. Filthy, malnourished, hungover, and sick as a dog from a batch of bad wine I'd greedily poured down my alcohol-raw throat."

Finding it harder and harder to equate David with the man he was describing, Matt could do no more than stare at him in astonishment.

Noting her expression, David smiled. "I know," he said. "It's hard to believe now, but I assure you every word is true."

"I wasn't doubting your veracity," Matt said. "No rational person would claim such a sordid past for mere shock value."

"And I am rational, have been for some time. Thanks to Rachel."

"You had to be a willing subject," Matt stated in

his defense. "Or even she couldn't have turned you around so completely."

"Perhaps," he conceded.

"So, after hauling you out of that alley, how did she go about assisting this transformation?"

"The first thing she did was dry me out." He winced. "It was awful...I hope never to have to live through anything like that again. With that boy's reproachful eyes looking on, my mind, every cell in my body, screamed for the anesthesia of alcohol."

Grimacing in remembrance, he shook his head.

"Go on," Matt urged.

"I'd have taken off at a run, of course, if I could have," he continued. "But there was this big guy holding me down—man that guy was big, strong as a bull elephant, yet gentle as a spring lamb." His features were softened by affection. "His given name was Dwain, but everybody called him 'The Train.'" He grinned. "For obvious reasons."

Despite the seriousness of the topic, his grin was so infectious, Matt couldn't contain a smile. "Were you in a detox center?"

"No." He shook his head. "At least, not an official one. I was in the dry-out room of Rachel's home—the home she had turned into a shelter. She had inherited the house, and a small monthly annuity," he explained. "Don't ask me how she managed to keep the place viable, but somehow she always did.

"Of course, Rachel did receive some help, in the form of donations from the residents in the area—some money, but not much, for they weren't even close to middle class. But they were fairly generous with foodstuffs, used clothing, soaps, toothpaste, things like that."

"Obviously, you weren't the only person who loved her," Matt observed.

"No, I wasn't the only one." His smile was so tender it caused an odd, unfamiliar ache in her chest. "Everybody young, old, and in between, inside and outside the shelter loved Rachel. She was living proof of the scripture of reaping what you sow."

"I'm glad she found you in that alley."

"I will be eternally grateful." He heaved a sigh.

He was quiet for a moment. Not wanting to intrude on his somber mood, Matt was quiet, too.

Then he smiled at Matt in a way that instantly lightened the atmosphere, and her spirits.

"And so, we finally get to the original point of this long story. Rachel didn't only run a shelter, she ran a soup kitchen. And she taught me to cook." He laughed in remembrance. "She was a fantastic cook—nothing fancy, but good, solid, nourishing food. She taught every person, man, woman or child who stayed at her shelter, to cook. I was no exception. When she deemed me ready, I did kitchen duty...with Rachel by my side, directing every move."

"She was a superb teacher," Matt said, smiling. "My grandmother and I can vouch for that."

"I liked your grandmother, Matt." He smiled.

"She liked you." She smiled back at him. "You, and your spaghetti sauce."

"The sauce recipe is Rachel's, not mine. She gets the credit." He grinned. "Every recipe I use is hers. But that's okay, because she gave me permission to do so when I left the shelter."

"And when was that?"

"Not quite a year after she hauled me into it." He hesitated a moment, then continued. "She had always told me I'd know when I was ready to leave."

"And did you?"

"Oh, yes, I knew."

Curious, Matt took what she believed to be a sure guess. "Because you had decided to go into the ministry?"

David smiled, but shook his head. "No, I had decided on the ministry a few months before leaving."

Stymied, Matt frowned. "Then, how?"

"I knew when that boy's eyes no longer reproached, but smiled at me before leaving me in peace."

"Oh, David," she whispered, blinking against the sting of tears in her eyes.

Chapter 7

"Here now, none of that," David said, giving her hand a quick squeeze before pushing his chair back. "We've been sitting here too long," he said decisively. "I think we both could use some fresh air and exercise."

"But..." Matt began. His final mention of a child's eyes, while touching her heart, also jogged her memory of the little girl she'd noticed in church.

"No buts," he said, striding to the closet for her coat and his jacket, then returning to circle the table to grasp her hands and pull her upright.

"But," she protested, laughing as he thrust her coat at her. "I thought of something, someone in church I wanted to ask you about."

"Concerning the desecration?"

"No," Matt said, slipping into her coat. "Not that. Just something I thought might be of interest to you...especially now, after hearing your story."

"Mmm, intriguing," he murmured, shrugging into his ski jacket and ushering her to the back door. "You can explain while we walk."

After the artificial heat of the house, the cold air was a shock...as was David's backyard. Shivering, Matt slid her hands into the side pockets of her long coat and looked around in delight. Though the only color in the sectioned garden came from a few lingering chrysanthemums and several evergreens, she could easily imagine how it must look in summer, with the many various plantings in full and glorious bloom.

David slanted a knowing look at her. "Still no gloves, hmm?"

Matt laughed, feeling the cold breeze against her teeth. "No," she admitted, shivering again.

"You're cold." He made a half turn. "We'll go back inside."

"No." Matt slipped her hand from her pocket to grasp his arm, halting him. "It was the shock. I'm fine. The cold air is refreshing. Let's walk." She motioned to the bricked pathways between the sections. "Did you design this garden?"

"Designed it and built it..." He laughed. "If 'build' is the correct term."

"Unimportant." Matt shrugged off the semantics. "I'm impressed. It's wonderful."

"Thanks." In a move so casual, it seemed the natural thing to do, he lifted her hand from his arm, threaded his fingers through hers, then started moving along the central pathway. "I like working with my hands, digging in the earth. It gives a man time to think."

"To ponder the mysteries of the universe?" Matt asked in a light, teasing tone. Her question was a bid to conceal her sudden attack of breathlessness caused by the warmth of his hand curled around hers.

He laughed. "Something like that."

What an incredible man, she mused, feeling her admiration for him go up another notch.

And what a complex man. In essence, three different and very distinct personalities, Matt reflected. The toughened soldier. The weakened derelict. The physically and morally strong, compassionate and determined pastor.

Add a garden builder, grower and philosopher into the bargain.

Incredible, indeed.

"The herb garden."

Until David spoke, drawing Matt from her reverie, she wasn't aware of staring at a straggly section of the garden.

"Oh...uh, I knew that." She hadn't; she hadn't

even *seen* the squared area. "My grandmother grows her own herbs, too." She rushed on, feeling rattled, and wondering why. "But Gram grows hers on a shelf attached to the kitchen windowsill."

"So do I, in the winter." He flicked a hand at the plot. "This is my summer herb garden."

"I...see." Matt cast her gaze around. "And that next little area?"

"Vegetables...also in the summer." Silent laughter lurked in his dry voice.

Matt gave him an arched look. "No kidding?"

He laughed. "Moving right along, folks." He tugged on her hand to get her moving. "To your left, you'll notice the rose garden...in repose now, of course, but a riot of colorful, sweet smelling blossoms in the summertime." He smiled and tilted his head up as a lone white flake landed on his nose. "When it isn't snowing, that is."

Matt surrendered to the urge to laugh.

David rewarded her with a light squeeze on her hand.

With the lacy white stuff swirling lazily around them, they continued their short tour in the same vein. David pointed out the wildflower patch, the still-blooming mums, and the boxwood hedges separating each individual section. The tour ended at the far end of the garden, under the scant protection of a huge, now bare-limbed old chestnut tree.

Matt looked through the branches at the whitish-gray sky. A frown tugged her eyebrows together.

"Are you cold?"

"No…a little concerned." She lowered her gaze to his eyes, struck anew by the depth of their dark blue color. "Gram's out visiting with friends. I hope this snowfall doesn't amount to anything."

"Are the friends responsible people?"

"Oh, yes." She nodded. "It's not that, it's just…" She shrugged.

"You worry." He ended her unfinished remark.

Matt's smile was faint. "Yes."

"Understandable," he said, his smile as warm as his hand, still clasping hers. "And commendable…but then, you're devoted to your family, aren't you?"

"Yes, certainly…but how do you know?"

He chuckled. "Oh, Officer Wolfe, your eyes glow with love whenever you speak of them."

"But…" Matt gave him a puzzled look. "The only family member I've mentioned is my grandmother."

"Not so." His lips curved into a chiding smile. "You mentioned them—briefly, I'll admit—on the night we met." Warm approval shaded his voice. "And your tone, your eyes, overflowed with sheer love for them."

"They're very special to me," Matt murmured, a bit self-conscious because of his praise.

"They should be." David's eyes darkened. "Until you've lost your loved ones, you can't know..." He stopped abruptly, took a deep breath, then went on. "Family should be the primary concern of everyone."

Sympathetic to the grief he obviously still suffered, Matt raked her mind for a topic to change the subject. Memory stirred, reminding her of the anxious concern in the eyes of the young girl in church that morning.

It wasn't exactly a change of subject, but she felt sure the information would distract David from his somber recollections.

"Speaking of families, David," she said, her tone as casual as she could manage. "Do you remember I told you I had made one observation during service this morning that I thought you should hear about?"

"Yes, of course." Bright interest chased the darkness of pain from his eyes. "An observation unconnected to the vandalism. Right?"

"That's right." Matt agreed. "There was this small family—a mother and two children. The boy was eighteen months or so, and the girl was eleven or twelve."

Matt went on to describe the three individuals in a concise, professional way. "It was the anxious expression on the girl's face, the fear in her eyes when her mother coughed, that caught my attention. And also, David, the woman looked ill and somehow desperate.''

Frowning in concentration, David slowly shook his head. ''From your description I can't place them... They're not regulars, I can tell you. I know my regulars.''

Matt didn't doubt that.

''But you can rest assured I'll look into it.'' His voice was strong with purpose. ''If the woman is ill and needs help, she'll receive it.''

Matt didn't doubt that, either.

Recalling the fear in the girl's eyes, the woman's pale, drawn face, Matt shivered with relief, then started at the sudden tug on her arm.

''Come along, Officer Wolfe. You're shivering again.'' He strode out from under the tree, taking her with him. ''Let's go back into the house and have some hot chocolate.''

Matt wasn't cold; not seriously cold. But she didn't argue the point. Hot chocolate had appeal.

It wasn't until they were seated once more at the table, steaming mugs of the rich drink in front of them, that Matt became uneasy in her mind.

The attraction she had felt for David at first sight, startling as it had been, paled in comparison to the myriad feelings stirring inside her now.

There was respect, which was fine. In her opinion, he had earned the respect of everyone who knew him.

There was admiration. Also fine. He possessed many admirable qualities.

Matt could deal with the first two feelings; it was the deeper, hidden feelings that scared her silly. There were emotional responses to him quaking through her, causing her to shiver in the warmth of the house.

There was a strong physical attraction Matt didn't even want to think about, never mind deal with. After her one and only adventure into the realm of the physical senses, which in truth had not been an adventure, but more a disappointing fiasco, she had consigned her natural sexual urges to the deep freeze. Those urges, seemingly never very strong to begin with, had remained frozen solid ever since.

Until now.

At some time, out there in David's winter-chilled garden, a spring thaw had set in inside Matt, reactivating her libido. And that wasn't fine.

But that wasn't even the worst of it. Matt was very much afraid her emotional responses to him ran even deeper than the physical.

She could fall in love with the man. Matt gulped a swallow of chocolate, never even noticing that the hot liquid seared her tongue.

Her gaze flicked to him; her heart performed a funny little thump-thump.

Oh, hell...she was in big trouble.

It was time for her to get out of there, Matt told herself. Past time. Way past time.

She didn't have time for love. Falling in love wasn't included in her agenda. It was strictly against her principles, her belief that being a cop, and being emotionally involved, was a dangerous combination. She had witnessed firsthand the proof of her beliefs in the fear revealed in the eyes of her mother, her aunts, no matter how hard they worked at concealment.

And Matt knew, as well, that, certainly clearer than she, her father and uncles had seen the fear, too. They'd seen it and lived with it every second they carried out their duties as law enforcement officers.

Yes, Matt reiterated to herself, it was time to get out of David's house, David's life.

He was dangerous to her.

Draining the still-hot drink that burned all the way down her throat, Matt set the mug on the table, pushed back her chair, and stood, ready to bolt.

Her abrupt action drew him from what appeared to be a reverie of his own—probably, she decided, concerning the mother and two children she had told him about.

"What's up?" he asked, smiling at her in a way that made her tremble inside.

"I've taken up enough of your day," she said briskly, damning the inner tremors. She started for the door on legs that were not as steady as she would have wished. "I'll be leaving now. But I'll be in touch if there's any new informa—"

"Wait a minute." He jolted up, shaking the table. "You can't leave now."

"Indeed?" Matt arched a brow.

"Yes, indeed." He mimicked her chilly tone. "And knock off the intimidating look." His eyes laughed at her. "I'm not impressed, because I've got your number."

"And what exactly does that mean?" She scowled.

He grinned, evidently still not impressed. "It means, my beautiful Officer Wolfe, that I know full well that you're an armor-plated marshmallow."

"What?" Matt frowned, at him, and the stupid thrill she got from hearing him call her beautiful. "What are you talking about?"

David laughed. "You. On the surface, you appear the tough, steel-encased cop. But I know that, inside, you're as soft and sweet as marshmallow."

"I am tough," she maintained, too firmly.

"Sure." His eyes fairly gleamed. "But my pot roast isn't."

"Huh?" Matt blinked. "Pot roast? What are you talking about? What pot roast?"

"The one I put together and shoved into the oven after church, for dinner," he explained.

After church? When after church? She had been

there after church; had come into the house with him after church. She hadn't seen him put together a pot roast and shove it into the oven.

Matt gave him the look. Her special look that usually preceded the command "Assume the position."

David laughed in the face of her *look*.

"Don't tell me you didn't notice how long it was taking me to prepare our lunch," he chided. "Or did you assume I'm just an extra-slow mover?"

Well, of course she had noticed. How could she have helped but notice? Matt recalled. But she did have some manners…she wouldn't have dreamed of commenting on what had seemed to be his lack of speed.

"Aha," he crowed. "Condemned by your own silence. I'll have you know that as a rule, I'm a veritable dervish in the kitchen. There's little time for fussiness or finesse when you're cooking for a horde of hungry street people and vagrants."

What could she say? Clueless, Matt fell back on humor. "A dervish, huh?"

"Well, that might be stretching it a bit," he conceded. "But I do make a great Yankee pot roast, if I must say so myself. And I made it just for you."

Matt knew when she was outflanked. He had cooked dinner for her…just for her. She accepted defeat with a inner sigh for herself, and a smile for him.

"All right, David. I'll stay for dinner."

"Good." His smile was bright with pleased satisfaction. "We'll eat about six. Okay?"

"Fine." Matt glanced at the clock. It was 1:37. "What do we do till then?"

"Get comfortable. Read the paper. Whatever." He shrugged and held out his hand. "Come on, you can help me build a fire."

David led Matt into the living room and to the fireplace. To her surprise, he actually did allow her to help him...she handed the wood to him. When he had the fire going, he stepped back and indicated the grouped chairs and sofa.

"Make yourself at home," he invited, moving to a wide, russet-colored velour lounge chair. "Kick your shoes off and relax."

Matt hesitated an instant, then, slipping out of her low-heeled pumps, curled up on the cream-and-green-striped sofa.

"Would you hand me the sports section of the paper, please?" He inclined his head. "It's there, at the other end of the sofa."

"Sure." Tilting to the side, she searched out the section and handed it to him.

"Thanks." He smiled; she fluttered. "You can have the rest...this will take me a while."

"Later, maybe," she murmured, absently staring into the flickering fire.

Quiet settled on the room, broken occasionally by the crackle of paper when he turned the page, and the softer crackle and pop of the burning wood. Mesmerized by the dancing flames, Matt cradled her head on the arm of the sofa. She was barely aware of the weight tugging on her eyelids.

She stirred at a light touch against her arm. Still half asleep, she opened her eyes to find David pulling an autumn-leaf-imprinted afghan over her.

"Sorry." His voice was soft, his eyes softer. "I didn't mean to wake you."

"'Sawright," she mumbled, raising a hand to cover a yawn.

"How long have I been asleep?" Without thought, she shifted onto her back and stretched out her legs.

"Not long. A half hour or so."

He was still bent over her; she could feel his breath feather her lips. Suddenly a hunger unrelated to pot roast sank its claws into her.

"I want to kiss you, Officer Wolfe." David's gravelly voice had lost its velvet coating. "I want to kiss you very badly."

"I—I hope you don't." Her voice was reedy, nearly nonexistent.

"Kiss you?" He sighed his disappointment.

"No," she whispered, a tremulous smile hovering on her lips. "I hope you don't kiss me very badly."

A flame brighter than any in the fireplace leaped in his eyes. His lips curved in a sensuous smile. He lowered his head; she caught the lingering scent of chocolate on his warm breath.

"You'll have to be the judge."

Matt heard his murmur an instant before she felt the light pressure of his mouth against hers.

Not yet fully awake, the taste of him, the excitement generated by his mouth molding to hers, sent her senses soaring into an altogether different realm of dreaming. It was Elysian. A paradise of pure blissful sensation.

With a low groan filling her mouth, David deepened the kiss. Matt raised her arms to coil them around his neck. His tongue glided along her bottom lip. Sighing, she opened, inviting the foray of his tongue.

Vaguely, Matt felt the afghan throw being whipped away, to be replaced by his weight. She felt the heat of him, the fullness of him, pressing into the material sheathing the juncture of her thighs.

Arching into him, she made a soft sound of frustration deep in her throat.

"I know the feeling," he murmured against her lips. "I want to touch you, kiss every inch of your soft skin." His voice roughened to a growl. "The clothes must go."

Sensation. Need. Raw desire burning away self-control, caution and inhibition. Matt surrendered to the moment, to her inner hunger...and to him.

"Yes."

Caught up in a haze of unleashed desire, the move was seamless from the living room to his bedroom. The first things to go were the pins anchoring her hair in a plait at the back of her head.

"Beautiful," he murmured, burying his hands in the gold-streaked mass. "I knew it would be."

Gently tugging on the long strands, he brought her mouth to his, not in demand, but in a mind-scattering seduction of her senses.

A searing flame of sheer sensation licking through her, Matt moaned and reached for him. At the same instant, he released her hair and reached for her. With trembling fingers—his and hers—the clothes were smoothed from quickening, quivering bodies.

David threw back the bedspread and covers.

Matt pulled him with her onto the bed.

With delightful, excruciating care, David fulfilled his wish to touch her, kiss every inch of her skin—which he declared both soft and silky.

In eager retaliation, Matt returned the pleasure given, lingering over the hardest, silkiest part of him.

"I...give up...Officer Wolfe..." He panted, compulsively arching into her caressing strokes. "I...can't...oh, have mercy, Matilda...I can't take any more."

Grasping her shoulders, he pulled her up the length of him. Matt shivered as the tips of her breasts brushed over the curls matting his chest, and the tip of his manhood brushed the curls matting her mound.

She let out a startled "Oh" when he heaved himself up and then over, taking her with him.

"I'll be with you in a moment," he promised in a passion whispery voice.

He reached over the side of the bed, and Matt heard him mutter to himself as he rummaged through a drawer in the nightstand, then exhale a deep sigh of relief. There came the sound of tearing foil. Matt watched as, leaning back, he sheathed himself in protection for them both.

The moments of separation could have been a cooling turnoff. Instead, watching him, empowered by the jutting proof of his desire for her, the flames of her desire for him turned into a roar.

Lowering himself to her once more, David cradled her face with his large, gentle hands, then crushed her mouth beneath his. His tongue teased her lips, avoiding her attempts to capture him, draw him inside.

Aroused to fever-pitch, Matt whimpered and arched into him in a silent demand.

Holding her lips with his, he slid his hands from her face, smoothing them slowly, maddeningly, down the sides of her body, pausing at every curve to stroke, to tease, to further inflame.

Her breathing shallow, Matt's hands mirrored his every caress. When his palms tested the smoothness of her inner thighs, her hands skimmed the bunched-muscled, hair-roughened texture of his.

When his fingers delicately dipped into the moist readiness of her femininity, her fingers curled around the fully aroused hardness of his masculinity.

His own breathing growing harsh, uneven, he reached for her hips...then grasped...then lifted... then thrust into her, with his body and his tongue.

Matt gasped at the galvanizing double thrill of pleasure and, craving more, eagerly matched his driving rhythm of parry and thrust.

The pleasure spun out; beautiful pleasure; unbearable pleasure, until, with a muffled cry, Matt attained the pinnacle of all pleasure.

She heard David's echoing cry a moment later.

Chapter 8

Something had awakened him.

Disoriented, not fully awake, Mac sat up in the bed, frowning, trying to figure out what had startled him. A sound...yes, that was it. Some sound had penetrated the depths of his satiated slumber, penetrated and set off an alarm inside him.

Matt.

Reality came back in a rush. He turned his head, knowing what he'd see...or, more accurately, who he wouldn't see.

Matt was gone. The sound that had awakened him had been the door being shut.

A sigh whispered into the quiet, dusk-shadowed room as Mac tossed the covers aside.

Even though he felt certain she was gone, he crawled out of bed and pulled on his boxers and jeans.

Maybe she had left a note.

Holding the hopeful thought, Mac, bare-chested and barefoot, left the room. Mere minutes were required to make a circuit of the house. There was no sign of a note anywhere.

Shoulders slumped in dejection, Mac stood in the middle of the kitchen, not noticing the chill from the floor tiles permeating the soles of his feet, or the fragrant aroma of pot roast scenting the air.

Why had she left without waking him?

Mac made a snorting sound. The answer was obvious: Matt didn't want to speak to him.

And why didn't she want to speak to him?

Also obvious, he reasoned. She must be suffering pangs of regret for their lovemaking.

Dammit.

Mac directed his gaze to the darkening sky beyond the window.

Sorry, Sir, he respectfully addressed his Creator. *But, You see, I don't understand. How could Matt regret the very same act I found so incredibly beautiful?*

I love her, he prayed, surprising himself with the truth he had not until now consciously acknowledged. *But, then, You knew that, didn't You?*

So, now what am I supposed to do? How do I

proceed? If by walking away without a word, Matt has rejected not only the reality of our lovemaking, but me, as well...

Mac closed his eyes and shuddered. He had never been in love. Oh, he had experienced heavy infatuation—and during the dark years, even heavier sexual indulgence—but never had he felt anything near the depth of caring, concern, excitement and thrill of the love he was feeling for Matt.

To have known her once, to have felt he had touched her mind and soul as well as her body, only to awaken alone...

No. Mac shook his head and opened eyes glittering with purpose. Determination straightened his spine and squared his drooping shoulders.

No, Sir. I can't...I won't simply allow her to walk away. I swear to You, on my pledge of service to You, that I will not harm her, physically or emotionally. But I can't believe that after giving herself to me in such joyous surrender, after the near perfection of our union, Matt does not care for me...love me.

In Your infinite wisdom, You know, I must know what she is feeling.

As always, having taken his problem, his concern, to the highest authority, Mac felt calmer.

She never would know if David's pot roast was as good as he claimed.

Standing under a pounding shower spray, tears running down her face, Matt sniffled, and told herself she had more important things to consider than a roasting piece of beef.

Things like deep-sixing every tenet and rule of personal conduct she had set for herself when she had decided on a career in law enforcement.

Things like her unexpected and unprecedented flash-fire response to him.

Things like her willing—no, eager—plunge into total abandonment to sensuality.

Things like the thrilling, unimaginable heights she had attained with David.

And, most frightening, most bewildering, things like the merging connectedness she had felt with him when they had soared together into ecstasy.

''Frightening'' barely described it.

Matt's shivering intensified.

She had never believed the oft-told tales of the blending of mind and soul as well as body supposedly experienced by lovers.

She had dismissed such recountings as the stuff of fictional fantasy, spun from the fertile imaginations of poets and writers of romantic novels.

Experiencing for herself the truth of those age-old tales, while momentarily glorious and uplifting, was sobering, almost chilling, with the ramifications inherent in the aftermath.

Switching off the cascading spray, Matt stepped

from the shower and wrapped herself in a towel. Her body quaked in reaction to the inner chill. She tossed back her wet-dark hair and glared at herself in the steam-clouded mirror.

She could do this, she told herself. She tried to stop her incipient sobs with hard repeated swallows. She could, and would, fight this unwanted, unasked-for development.

She loved David...was in love with David.

There, she'd admitted it.

It didn't change a thing.

Being in love weakened her.

She was a cop, dammit.

David was an ordained minister.

And the pairing of the cop and the pastor could not be a happening thing.

It wouldn't work.

Which meant, her work was cut out for her.

Which meant, she had to work at cutting him from her heart, her thoughts, her life.

Ignoring the shaft of pain the decision sent spearing into her chest, Matt dumped the sodden towel into the hamper. Stepping into her nightclothes, she strode from the bathroom to the kitchen.

She was amazed when a glance at the wall clock told her that less than an hour had elapsed since she had left David. Since she had crept, shattered and trembling, from David's bed, then his house, unable to face him in the afterglow of their soul-stirring lovemaking.

Figuring her grandmother wouldn't be home for another hour or two, she dashed off a terse note, saying she was home, and had gone to catch a nap before starting her shift at midnight. Then, assured she would not be disturbed by her loving grandparent, she went to her bedroom, crawled between the sheets, and curled into a ball of pure, unadulterated misery.

Her throat tight with trapped sobs, Matt silently repeated her new mantra over and over again.

I can do this.

It was going to be a very long night, Matt predicted as she crawled from her bed. Long and boring. As a rule, the Sunday night shift was quiet and uneventful. For Matt, she somehow knew this night wouldn't prove the exception.

She hadn't slept, of course. She had heard her grandmother come home, putter about. She had feigned sleep when she'd heard Gram mount the stairs and open her door a sliver to peek in on her. She had heard the muted sounds issuing from the TV.

Matt had lain on her personal bed of nails until the last possible minute, allowing her only time enough to prepare for work.

She was uniformed, her hair smoothed back in her

usual plait, applying an extra coat of concealing un-
dereye makeup when her grandmother tapped on the
door.

"Come on in, Gram," she called in a casual tone
she was light-years from feeling. "I'm almost
ready."

"Have a good nap, dear?" Maddy asked, standing
in the open doorway.

"Not really." Matt pulled off a creditable shrug
and smile. "But then, I never do on the first night
of this shift…as I'm sure you know."

"Too well." She nodded, her smile bittersweet.
"I lived through it, first with your grandfather, then
your uncle Jake…and now with you."

"You're a tolerant, patient and wonderful woman,
Gram," Matt said, love for the woman plain in her
voice. Giving a final swish of the blusher brush to
her cheeks to camouflage the pallor, she turned, a
genuine smile on her still unsteady lips. "I often
wonder how—and why—you put up with all of us."

Maddy's washed-out blue eyes twinkled with inner amusement.

"I'm rather fond of my oversize bunch," she
drawled. "Besides, looking after all of you keeps me
off the street and out of trouble."

Matt laughed, even though it hurt her throat.

"I have fresh coffee ready for you." Maddy's
voice was brisk. "How about some eggs?"

Matt's stomach heaved. "Ah…no, thanks."

"Cereal?" Maddy, a firm believer of a solid meal before going to work, persisted.

"I'm really not hungry, Gram." Matt swallowed the sour taste in her mouth. "I'll just have coffee."

Maddy leveled a stern look on her. "You should have something in your stomach besides coffee."

Too tired to argue, Matt sighed and relented. "Okay, I'll have toast."

"Toast," Maddy grumbled, turning away. "Well, I suppose it's better than nothing."

With her grandmother watching her like the legendary hawk, Matt managed to force down two pieces of toast.

"By the way," Maddy said, after settling into the chair opposite Matt. "I didn't see you in church this morning. Did you cop out, no pun intended—" she grinned, sweeping a glance over Matt's uniformed torso "—or did you decide to attend services at David's church, after all?"

"I attended David's service," she said, nearly choking on a bite of toast.

"Well?" Maddy prompted when Matt didn't elaborate. "How was it?"

"He gives a very good sermon," she said, reflecting it was probably better if one actually heard it.

"I like that man," Maddy said decisively.

Matt cringed inside. "So you said before."

Though she had thought she'd kept her tone free

of inflection, something in her voice must have alerted the older woman, for she frowned.

"You don't like David?"

No, I love him.

Naturally, Matt wasn't about to voice the first response that sprang into her beleaguered mind.

"Yes, of course I like him," she answered. "What's not to like about him?" Indeed, she added to herself, feeling the toast like lead in her stomach.

"I'll have to invite him over sometime," Maddy said in a musing tone. "Give him a taste of my cooking."

Oh, God. Matt quailed at the mere suggestion. Afraid she'd betray herself at any minute, she scraped back her chair and stood.

"Gotta go, Gram," she said, shoving her arms into her jacket sleeves, then scooping her holstered weapon from the corner of the table. "I'll see you in the morning," she rushed on, making for the back door. "Sleep well…and don't worry."

"Why should I change my habits at this late date?" Maddy retorted. "Take care."

Now, after the long night hours of tooling her squad car along empty streets and battling the yearning ache that slammed into her every time she drove past the turnoff to the church and David's house beyond, Matt recalled her grandmother's parting remark with wry cynicism.

"Take care of what?" she asked herself. She glanced at the dashboard clock, not for the first, or even thirty-first time since she'd begun her patrol.

The clock read seven-twenty. Just forty minutes remained of her shift.

"Four-one?"

Matt started at the crackling summons—the first in a long while—and groaned. Sure. Why not? she groused to herself. Far be it for the fates to let her get through the entire night without a major incident.

Resigned, she reached for the handset.

"Four-one," she repeated.

"Where are you located?"

"I'm just leaving the college circle, heading north on Elm," she responded. "What's up?"

"We've received a report of a desecration of church property on..."

No. Matt shook her head as the voice continued to crackle particulars. Not even the most fickle of fates could be this mean-spirited, she railed.

But, of course, the church property in question was David's domain.

For an instant, just a millisecond, rebellion flared inside Matt, then she just as quickly squashed it. She had realized she'd have to face him sometime.... But, hell, did it have to be at 7:25 in the morning? This morning, of all mornings?

"I'm on it," she responded, sighing as she replaced the handset.

Taking the fastest route, Matt cruised along the silent streets, inwardly girding herself for whatever she might have to endure when she saw David.

He was waiting on the road next to the crèche. From his surprised reaction when she stepped from the car, it was obvious he'd not been expecting her to respond.

"More paint, David?" she asked, miraculously managing to keep her voice crisp, cool and professional.

He moved closer to her. "Matt..." He reached for her hand. "We've got to talk about—"

"I'm on duty, Reverend," she interrupted, stepping aside to avoid his touch.

"I know that, but—"

"Let's see the damage." She again cut him off. Taking two steps to get a closer look at the wooden figures, she remained far enough back so as not to disturb any possible footprints in the ground which had been softened by the fitful snowfall the previous afternoon.

"You didn't..."

"No I didn't," David said over her voice. "As you'll notice, you don't have to be on top of it to see the strange handiwork of the vandal."

Matt could hardly believe what she saw. She stared in astonishment at the sight before her.

"Weird, wouldn't you say?" David said, coming to a halt beside her.

"Look on the bright side," Matt muttered, moving one step closer to the scene—and away from him. "At least there's no black paint to remove this time."

"True. All I have to do is pull that black trash bag from the figure of the Virgin Mary." He grimaced. "Of course, we don't know what's underneath the bag."

"Live in hope," Matt muttered one of her grandmother's sayings.

"Oh, I do." His voice held a wealth of meaning.

Matt chose to misunderstand his remark. "What is it with this perp?" she mused out loud. "First a spray of black paint to obliterate the figure's face, now a black bag over its head." She frowned. "I'm beginning to wonder if this could be the work of some cult member."

"I've been wondering the same thing ever since I noticed it around seven," he said, allowing her to get away with the diversionary tactic.

"On the other hand...you know..." Matt slanted a sidelong look at him. "If it wasn't for the proof of your big feet—" her glance came to rest on the large-size running shoes "—I might be tempted to consider you a suspect."

David's dark blue, amusement-filled eyes were waiting to pierce her when she slowly returned her gaze to his face. "No kidding?" he drawled. "And might I ask why you might be so tempted?"

She lifted her shoulders in half shrug. "Well, considering the strangeness of the hours you happen to notice the vandalism…the first one not long before midnight, and now so early in the morning—" She broke off, shrugging again.

"If you'll recall, I explained about the first incident. I was on my way home from visiting a parishioner." He smiled. "You've met Corine Baxter. She can tell you the exact time I left her house."

His mention of the blond woman's name caused an odd, unpleasant sensation in Matt's midsection—certainly not jealously, she assured herself. But what had he been doing at the other woman's home until after eleven o'clock that night, anyway?

"And this morning?" She arched her brows, dismissing Corine from her unsettling thoughts.

"This morning, Officer Wolfe," he said in a gritty voice, "I was attempting to walk off my frustration after a long, sleepless night."

"Oh." Beating a hasty retreat, Matt returned to the car to call base and request a lab crew.

As he had done days before, David was right behind her. He slid into the seat, right beside her.

"You're damned right, 'Oh,'" he said, slamming the passenger door. "Why did you run—no, sneak out on me without a word of explanation, or so much as a 'see ya, fella,' yesterday afternoon, Matt?"

"I'm on duty, Reverend," she repeated, using the

excuse as a shield against him. "I can't talk now. I have to tape off the—"

"Bull," he retorted, slicing through her attempt to evade his question. "I helped you do that before, if you'll remember. It only took a few seconds. And it'll take a while for the lab crew to get here."

"David, I prefer not to discuss this now," she said, inwardly battling a resurgence of the shivers.

"I need to know, Matt," he persisted, grasping her arm as she moved to step out of the car.

Although his hold on her arm was gentle, it was firm. Nevertheless, Matt made a point of lowering her gaze to his hand, then raising narrowed eyes to his.

"Let me go, David." Her voice was soft in tone, but hard in authority.

"Sorry, Officer." He gave a quick shake of his head. "I need to know why you left my bed, my house, and me, after the incredibly beautiful experience we shared."

The inner shivers had matured into wrenching quakes, threatening to tear her apart and expose her true feelings, her love for him. Determined to conceal her emotions, she withdrew behind a brittle facade.

"We had sex," she said.

"We made love," he corrected her in sharp, impatient tones. "I made love to you, and deny it now if you dare, you made love to me."

"No…I…"

"Yes, Matt," he persisted, hammering at her already weakened defenses. "I know, I was there, and fully involved. And…so…were…you," he said, spacing each damning word for emphasis. "And I want to stay involved with you. And not only to make love." He took a quick breath, then hammered relentlessly on. "Now I'll ask you again, why did you leave me without a word of explanation?"

Matt was nearly undone. This was worse than she had feared. It was bad enough that she was in love with him, but he was indicating, or at least hinting, that he was in love with her.

And she was convinced that any serious involvement—and he sure sounded serious—would definitely be unfair…to him.

She had been there, grown up in the midst of such involvements. Loving an officer of the law inflicted terror and mental torment along with its inherent joys and rewards.

No. David was too good, too fine a man to subject to that kind of uncertainty. He had suffered too much already. He deserved better, more than she could offer or guarantee.

She had set her course; she'd stay it.

"Let me go, David," she ordered, pulling against his grip. "I have to tape…"

"Answer me, Matt."

"I don't want to be involved, okay?" Matt

shouted back at him, barely hanging on to what was
left of her composure. "Yes, our lovemaking was
wonderful...more than that," she admitted, the
quakes inside working their way to the surface. "But
it should not have happened. I lost my head for a
while..." Her voiced hardened. "It won't happen
again."

"But why?" David shook his head, as if clearing
the effects of a blow. "Matt, didn't you hear, understand? I'm not looking for a brief period of fun
and games. I'm telling you that I'm in lo—"

"Don't say it," she shouted, drowning him out.
"I don't want to hear it." She gasped a harsh breath.
"You have no idea what being involved with a law
enforcement officer entails. I do. I have lived with it
each and every day of my life."

"I don't care about that," David said when she
paused for another gasp of air. "I care about you. I
care about us. I don't care about—"

"I care enough for both of us." She again sliced
through his words. "I must. I will not subject you,
or any other man, to that kind of gut-wrenching,
emotion-ripping uncertainty." Tearing free of him,
she slid from the seat.

"Matt, wait," David demanded, flinging the door
open and zipping around the car to her. "Listen..."

"The discussion is over, Reverend." Drawing
herself up to her full height, she stared into his eyes,

and coldly, deliberately, cut him off at the knees. "The subject is closed."

Turning her back to him, feeling as though she was crumbling into tiny painful, sharp-edged shards inside her rigid frame, Matt strode to meet the police car coming up the driveway.

Chapter 9

Matt was tired, more tired than she could ever remember feeling. Her weariness was understandable, considering the amount of sleep she'd clocked, or more accurately, hadn't clocked; she had spent most of her time in bed tossing and turning. But at least her stint on the late-night shift was finally over.

As she had suspected would be the case, the lab crew had come up with little more evidence than before regarding the desecration. Instead of one, this time there had been two sneaker toe imprints, made by either a child or a short, slender adult. There had not been a print or any other mark on the figure under the bag.

In Matt's unvoiced opinion, the perp had been an

adult, a young adult. Possibly a teenager who'd either held a grudge against David or the church, or had committed the crime for the sheer, upset-causing hell of it. She'd had occasions to deal with her share of such teenagers.

Not eager for another confrontation with David—and because she ached too much to see him—Matt asked the officer working the day shift patrol on that route to stop by to bring David up to speed on the case.

Her week was in. And now she was on official vacation leave until after the holidays.

Christmas was just four days away, and she was anticipating the arrival of her immediate and extended family.

Dragging her sleep-depleted body from her cover-rumpled bed, Matt padded barefoot down the stairs to the kitchen for a hopefully reviving cup of coffee. She found her grandmother there, in the process of baking Christmas goodies…again.

"What is it this time, Gram?" Matt asked, smothering a yawn with her hand. "Not more cookies?"

"No." Maddy glanced up from the pastry rolled out on the tabletop to smile at her. "I'm baking those little pecan tarts your uncle Royce loves."

"Him and everybody else," Matt said, grinning as she made a beeline for the coffeemaker.

"Coffee's fresh," Maddy said, laying the rolling pin aside to begin cutting out small circles of pastry with a scalloped-edged cookie cutter. "I started it when I heard you moving around upstairs."

"You're a lifesaver," she vowed fervently, taking a mug from the cup tree on the countertop and filling it with the fragrant brew.

"And you look like you need saving," Maddy retorted, peering into Matt's face. "Are you coming down with something?"

"No, Gram, I'm just tired. You know I never sleep well when I'm on the late shift."

"Yes, I do know," she nodded, frowning. "But you look even more washed out than usual this time."

"Well…I suppose I'm a little excited about Mom, Dad and Lisa coming tomorrow," Matt quickly improvised, forgiving herself because she *was* eager for their arrival. "Maybe I'm not as grown-up as I like to believe."

Maddy chuckled. "Then that makes two of us kids, honey, because I'm just as excited as you are."

Matt laughed, then sat quietly, sipping her coffee and watching as the older woman swiftly put the little tarts together. Impressed by her grandmother's dexterity and talent—the woman was an excellent cook—Matt's mind drifted in the direction of another excellent cook. She wondered if David had bothered to prepare any special foods for the holiday, or if he had gotten around to putting up a tree for

An Important Message from the Editors

Dear Reader,

Because you've chosen to read one of our fine romance novels, we'd like to say "thank you!" And, as a **special** way to thank you, we've selected <u>two more</u> of the books you love so well **plus** an exciting Mystery Gift to send you — absolutely <u>FREE</u>!

Please enjoy them with our compliments...

Pam Powers

How to validate your Editor's "Thank You" FREE GIFT

1. Peel off gift seal from front cover. Place it in space provided at right. This automatically entitles you to receive 2 FREE BOOKS and a fabulous mystery gift.

2. Send back this card and you'll get 2 brand-new *Romance* novels. These books have a cover price of $5.99 or more each in the U.S. and $6.99 or more each in Canada, but they are yours to keep absolutely free.

3. There's no catch. You're under no obligation to buy anything. We charge nothing—ZERO—for your first shipment. And you don't have to make any minimum number of purchases—not even one!

4. The fact is, thousands of readers enjoy receiving their books by mail from The Reader Service. They enjoy the convenience of home delivery...they like getting the best new novels at discount prices BEFORE they're available in stores... and they love their Heart to Heart subscriber newsletter featuring author news, horoscopes, recipes, book reviews and much more!

5. We hope that after receiving your free books you'll want to remain a subscriber. But the choice is yours— to continue or cancel, any time at all! So why not take us up on our invitation, with no risk of any kind. You'll be glad you did!

GET A *Free* MYSTERY GIFT...

SURPRISE MYSTERY GIFT COULD BE YOURS **FREE** AS A SPECIAL "THANK YOU" FROM THE EDITORS

DETACH AND MAIL CARD TODAY!

Yes! I have placed my

Editor's "Thank You" seal in the
space provided above. Please
send me 2 free books and a
fabulous mystery gift. I
understand I am under no
obligation to purchase any
books, as explained on the
back and on the opposite page.

PLACE
FREE GIFT
SEAL
HERE

393 MDL DVFG   193 MDL DVFF

FIRST NAME   LAST NAME

ADDRESS

APT.#   CITY

STATE/PROV.   ZIP/POSTAL CODE

(PR-R-04)

Thank You!

The Reader Service — Here's How It Works:

Accepting your 2 free books and gift places you under no obligation to buy anything. You may keep the books and gift and return the shipping statement marked "cancel." If you do not cancel, about a month later we'll send you 3 additional books and bill you just $4.74 each in the U.S., or $5.24 each in Canada, plus 25¢ shipping & handling per book and applicable taxes if any.* That's the complete price and — compared to cover prices starting from $5.99 each in the U.S. and $6.99 each in Canada — it's quite a bargain! You may cancel at any time, but if you choose to continue, every month we'll send you 3 more books, which you may either purchase at the discount price or return to us and cancel your subscription.

*Terms and prices subject to change without notice. Sales tax applicable in N.Y. Canadian residents will be charged applicable provincial taxes and GST.

If offer card is missing write to: The Reader Service, 3010 Walden Ave., P.O. Box 1867, Buffalo, NY 14240-1867

BUSINESS REPLY MAIL
FIRST-CLASS MAIL   PERMIT NO. 717-003   BUFFALO, NY

POSTAGE WILL BE PAID BY ADDRESSEE

THE READER SERVICE
3010 WALDEN AVE
PO BOX 1341
BUFFALO NY 14240-8571

NO POSTAGE
NECESSARY
IF MAILED
IN THE
UNITED STATES

the decorations she'd seen littering his dining room table.

"Well, that's the first batch in," Maddy said, scattering Matt's errant thoughts. "Now, I'm going to take a coffee break before starting another batch."

"Good," Matt said, groping for a normal tone of voice, and an unaffected smile.

Pull it together, Wolfe, she chastised herself, annoyed with herself for her thinking of David every time she relaxed her guard.

"You have any plans for today?"

Jolted from her musings once more, Matt concealed her chagrin behind her mug. She drained the reviving liquid before responding to her grandmother's question.

"I need to finish my Christmas shopping," she said, rising to refill her mug. "Why, was there something you wanted me to do for you?"

"No." Maddy shook her head. "I was just wondering. Everything's under control here."

Her assertion elicited an easy laugh from Matt. "When don't you have everything under control, Gram?" she asked, a teasing smile curving her lips.

"I've had a lot of practice, honey," Maddy retorted. "Over sixty years of practice."

"And practice makes perfect?"

"Not always." Maddy smiled. "It helps if one's paying attention."

Something she hadn't been doing much of the past

week or so, Matt acknowledged ruefully. She really did need to forget one too attractive, too tempting, too exciting man of the cloth, and get her act together.

Starting now.

Her resolve in place, Matt finished her drink, rinsed her mug, then headed for her bedroom with purposeful strides. "I'm gonna get dressed and get going, Gram," she said over her shoulder. "Make a list, if there's anything I can pick up for you."

"I'll think of something." Maddy's teasing response followed her along the hallway.

The mall was packed. Canned holiday music serenaded the harried-looking shoppers. Bright-eyed youngsters waited in line with eager anticipation to sit on the knee of the red-suited man to recite their list of wants.

Matt loved it all. She always had. She was one of a handful of people she knew who didn't groan whenever she heard some version or other of "White Christmas."

Since her own childhood, Christmas had been a magical time, a time of belief in the possibility of miracles. Attaining adulthood had not tarnished the special wonder of the holiday for her. Not even the harsh realities of her job had changed her feelings.

Matt didn't rush along with the horde. Absorbing the sights and sounds, she strolled the broad walkway, admiring the window displays and decorations. The green and red displays would disappear all too quickly in the New Year, replaced by cupids with bows and arrows, big red hearts, roses of every hue, and yards of trailing white lace. But that was okay. Matt liked Valentine's Day, too.

Toting an oversize shopping bag with an enlarged face of Santa Claus on the side, Matt had made every purchase on her grandmother's list, and all but one of her own. She still hadn't quite decided on a gift for her father—the man was difficult to buy for.

She was perusing the items displayed in the window of a men's store when her glance came to a halt on a loden green and white sweater.

David. The garment fairly shouted his name to her. David would look terrific in that sweater.

You're losing it, lady, Matt scathingly told herself. She dragged her gaze from the sweater—and her rebellious mind from the man.

Dad. Remember? Matt chided herself. She directed her gaze to the other articles displayed. What to get for the legendary Lone Wolfe?

In the end, Matt surrendered to whimsy. A hint of a devilish smile twitching the corners of her mouth, she selected an outrageously expensive silk dressing gown for the man who never even wore pajamas, never mind a robe.

Matt exited the mall with a jaunty stride, humming a refrain of ''Jingle Bells.''

* * *

David anchored the gold star to the topmost branch of the live blue spruce. Descending the ladder, he folded it and set it aside. After plugging in the tiny lights, he stepped back to admire his handiwork.

Beautiful, he decided...wishing Matt were there to admire it with him.

Over a week had passed since their contentious conversation. A week during which Mac had upbraided himself for giving in too easily to Matt's dictum, and condemning her for her lack of faith in him, his ability to deal with the dangerous aspects of her career.

He'd expected Matt to drop by to tell him the results of the lab report, as she had before. Mac had held out hope of coaxing her into the house, then taking the opportunity to convince her that his love for her was strong enough to withstand the uncertainties of being the mate of a law enforcement officer.

His hopes were dashed when earlier in the week the officer who had stepped from the squad car in front of his house had turned out to be a man.

Mac knew himself to be a patient man...he had acquired the quality the hard way. But he also recognized the warning symptoms when his patience rope was about played out. He had just about reached that point.

Staring at the star until it blurred around the edges, Mac sought comfort from his Supreme superior.

I'm pushing the patience envelope, Sir, running close to desperate. Loving her the way I do, I must see her, or at least call her, try to make her understand.

Mac heaved a sigh, then continued on in his silent communication.

I don't suppose You could find the time to whisper an encouraging word in her ear, perhaps? Or if not that, infuse her with a little spirit of the season of giving…maybe?

He blinked, and the star refocused in his sight.

Arrogant jerk, he derided himself, grimacing as he turned away. As if the Lord didn't have enough to contend with in the world. Where did he get off, bothering the Boss with his personal, emotional problems? Didn't the Bible say God helps those who help themselves?

With a rueful shake of his head, Mac picked up the ladder and started from the room. Then he stopped to pause, a serene smile softening the thin line of his lips.

Of course.

As often happened, Mac was struck by the wonderful and mysterious ways of the Lord…. Who helped those who helped themselves.

His purpose firm, he went straight to the phone.

Maddy answered.

After exchanging greetings with the young-at-heart older woman, Mac asked for Matt.

"She's not here, Mac, I sent her out for some last-minute grocery items." Maddy laughed. "I had thought I'd remembered everything I needed for the holidays," she went on chattily, bringing a tender smile to his lips. "But then I remembered that Matt's mother and sister prefer fresh lime in their seltzer water, and me with a crisper full of lemons."

Mac laughed along with her, but then his brows drew together in a frown. "That's right, Matt told me her family would be visiting for the holidays...from Colorado, right?"

"Yes." Barely suppressed excitement shimmered in her voice. "They arrive tomorrow. Matt's driving to Philadelphia International to pick them up."

"I'll bet she's anxious to see them."

"Anxious hardly describes it," Maddy said, chuckling. "She's been like a whirlwind these past few days—shopping, wrapping, cleaning an already-clean house, and getting underfoot, like a windup toy."

Mac wanted to see her like that. Her cool reserve, her professional facade stripped away to reveal the warm and loving woman beneath.

"Well..." He closed his eyes and smothered a sigh. "You have a lovely Christmas, Maddy. You and Matt, and your family. I'll—"

"I'll have Matt return your call, Mac," she cut in to promise. "As soon as she comes in."

"No, she's busy," he said, certain she would definitely be too busy to listen to his plea. "I'll get ba—"

"Mac?" Maddy again cut him off.

"Yes, Maddy?"

"I know you must have a full schedule, and I'll understand if you can't, but..." She hesitated, as if unsure about continuing.

"What can I do for you, Maddy?" he asked gently.

"Well...I really would like you to meet my family," she explained. "If you could find time—if only for a few minutes—would you stop by the house on Christmas night when they'll all be here?"

Mac didn't hesitate for an instant. "Thank you for the invitation, Maddy. I'd like to meet your family. Would early in the evening be convenient?"

"That will be fine, Mac." Her voice was shades lighter. "I'll be looking forward to seeing you then."

It wasn't until after he had hung up the receiver that Maddy's phrasing registered. She had said they would all be there. Exactly how many Wolfe family members were there?

Then he shrugged. Made no difference. His primary interest was in one particular Wolfe, the she-Wolfe in cop's clothing.

*   *   *

Matt was having a wonderful time. She knew she was. She told herself so at least once an hour. She always had a wonderful time when the family was together. Yet this year, some of the shine was off the holiday glow.

The house was bedlam. But then, the house was always bedlam when the family gathered to celebrate anything—a holiday, a birthday, an anniversary, or just simply being together.

It was late in the afternoon. Christmas was almost over. The gifts had been opened, exclaimed over and, in the case of Matt's father, Cameron, hooted over by his three brothers.

The men, Maddy's four sons and six of her eight grandsons, were in the kitchen, where they usually convened, because the beer was there.

The females of the family were relaxing in the living room, resting between the chores of serving then clearing away the remains of a huge traditional Christmas dinner, before some male decided it was time for a snack.

Sipping from a chilled glass of Chardonnay, Matt was enjoying a friendly argument with her sister over an obscure point of law when the doorbell rang.

"I'll get that," she volunteered, since she was seated nearest to the door.

People had been stopping by all day to say hello and offer holiday wishes. Expecting another neighbor or friend, Matt swung the door open, and froze, the words "Merry Christmas" withering on her tongue.

Before her, in the flesh—the pulse-leaping flesh— stood the very reason her day hadn't turned out as wonderful as she had anticipated it would.

"David." Less than a whisper, his name passed her lips on a breathy sigh.

"Merry Christmas, Matt." He didn't smile, just stood there, a large cardboard carton in his arms.

"Mac! Come in, come in," Maddy called, bustling to the door, her smile for him changing to a chiding frown for Matt. "It's cold out there."

"Thank you, and Merry Christmas," he repeated the greeting as he stepped inside. "And this is for you." He extended his arms, offering the carton to her. "Don't worry, it isn't heavy."

Maddy's smile held puzzlement and pleased surprise as she accepted the gift. "But whatever..."

"Why don't you open it and see, Grandmother?" The advice came in an amused drawl from Matt's sister Lisa, who had come to stand beside Maddy.

Brief as it was, Matt saw the fleeting expression of shock that flashed on David's face and in his eyes. Then, just as swiftly, the expression changed to comprehension and amusement.

"Twins," he murmured, his gaze probing Matt's. "You're identical twins."

"Yes." She nodded, looking cool, feeling hot.

"Lisa, this is the Reverend David Macdonough. He's fairly new to the area." She mentioned the name and location of his church. "David, my sister Lisa."

"A pleasure, David," Lisa said, flashing her perfect white teeth as she extended her hand. "But...didn't my grandmother call you Mac?"

"The pleasure's mine, Lisa. And I'm Mac to some, David to...others." He smiled and shifted his glance from her to Matt. "Are you a cop, too?"

"Not I." Lisa grinned. "I'm a lawyer."

"Figures."

At that point, having opened the carton and removed the white freezer paper covering the contents, Maddy exclaimed, "Oh, my goodness! Mac, did you bake these?"

Naturally, her question sharpened the interest of the other four women in the room. Exchanging curious glances, after they left their chairs to have a look.

"It's bread," said Sarah, Jake's wife.

"It's a lot of bread," said Megan, Royce's wife.

"It's a lot of different kinds of bread," added Tina, Eric's wife, and the avid cook of the group.

"They smell divine," said Sandra, Cameron's wife, and Lisa and Matt's mother.

"You baked these?" It was a chorus, combined of every female voice there—but Matt's. She was otherwise occupied hanging David's coat in the closet.

"Yes," David answered, his eyes sparkling with delight for the friendly women. "It's my contribution to Maddy...and her family."

"Mac, thank you, this is wonderful," Maddy said, lifting one of the individually plastic-wrapped loaves from the carton. "Italian bread. I love it."

"I know," David said, laughing at the confused look she gave him. "The church supper, remember?"

"And a batch of corn bread, my favorite," Megan said, taking another package from the box.

"Oh-hh, a long loaf of French," Sarah announced. "Jake's gonna devour this."

"Navajo fry bread!" Sandra laughed. "I haven't had that in forever."

"Look at this." Tina held an iced loaf aloft. "Stollen. I've never had success with stollen."

Of course, Lisa had to discover the last of the breads. "And Greek braided bread." She tossed a smile at David. "This is some multinational contribution."

"I lived in a multinational neighborhood for a while," David replied, sliding a conspiratorial look at Matt.

Suddenly remembering her manners, Maddy introduced David to her family. Then, carefully replacing the bread in the carton, she handed it to Matt.

"Matt take the bread, and Mac, into the kitchen, and introduce him to your father, uncles and cousins."

"How many uncles and cousins are there?" David murmured as they moved through the dining room.

"Three uncles, only six of the cousins," she answered. "Two of my cousins couldn't make it. This was their year to spend the holidays with their wives' families."

"And didn't you say that all of them are in law enforcement?"

Matt gave a brief nod. "Except my mother and Lisa, they're both lawyers," she said tersely, heading toward the sound of male voices and laughter. "Brace yourself," she warned. "They're a bit of a surprise."

Surprise was a woefully inaccurate description, Mac decided minutes later, upon coming face-to-face with a roomful of handsome blond giants.

It wasn't their height that struck him; not one of them topped him by more than an inch. Nor was it their male good looks that gave him pause. No, what most impressed Mac was the keen intelligence and bright humor that gleamed from the depths of the ten pairs of eyes that turned to assess him when he followed Matt into the kitchen.

And the sharpest of those eyes belonged to the oldest member of the group, Mac quickly discovered when he was introduced to Cameron Wolfe, Matt's father.

The man's grip might have been crushing...if Mac hadn't been able to match it.

The humor in Cameron's eyes spread to his lips and voice. "Nice to meet you, Reverend."

After apparently passing muster with Matt's father, meeting the others was a piece of cake. Although keeping the names straight was chancy.

There were the uncles, Royce, Eric and Jake. And the cousins, Justin, Edward, Andrew, Tim, Todd and Brian. Mark and Jeffrey were the two missing cousins.

"Baked all these yourself, did you?"

Mac thought the voice with the hint of ridicule came from Edward, Royce's son. He found a moment later that he'd guessed right.

"Don't knock it, son," Royce chastised his firstborn. "A man who can bake his own bread will never starve."

"I'll bet Tina freaked when she saw this." Eric displayed the stollen.

"And I'll bet Sandra's mouth watered when she spied the fry bread—she loves it," Cameron said, sharing a grin with his brother.

"What can we get you to drink, Reverend?" Jake asked, eyeing the long loaf of French bread.

"Name's Mac...or David," he said. "And I'll have a soda, thank you."

"Comin' up." Jake grinned, revealing yet another set of pearly whites. "Justin, get Mac a soda."

Within minutes, to Mac's heartfelt gratitude, the Wolfe males had drawn him into their very serious and highly contentious discussion on the pros and cons of the two teams most likely to go to the Super Bowl.

By ten that evening, it was pretty evident to Matt that every one of her family members, male and female alike, had taken to David's easygoing manner, his humor, and his obvious affection for people in general.

He had been invited to join the family for supper. A minor thing to some, perhaps, but a major consideration to Matt. It broke new ground, insofar as family suppers had always before been limited to actual family members.

But that wasn't even the worst of it. Matt suspected each and every one of her family members of indulging in a bit of matchmaking. The match being between her and David, of course. And her suspicions were not without reason or merit. She was wise to the little hints, the casual nuances, the offhand remarks—ostensibly made in jest—about how good they looked at one point while they were standing together.

Her suspicions were confirmed when, around ten-thirty, David made noises about leaving. Everyone suggested that Matt escort him to the door.

"Perfect," David murmured as soon as they were out of the room, and earshot. "I need to talk to you."

Harboring warring emotions of frustration at having to spend even a few minutes alone with him, and excitement at getting to spend even a few minutes alone with him, she led the way along the hall to the front door in a state of cool and withdrawn composure.

She was expecting him to renew his attack on her position of no involvement.

David surprised her.

"I located the woman and children you mentioned to me about noticing in church the other week." He smiled, as if aware of having thrown her a curve. "She lives about a quarter of a mile down the road from the church."

"Along my patrol route?"

"Yes."

"Is she ill...in trouble?" Matt asked, vividly recalling the woman's pallor, the anxious expression on the young girl's face.

"Yes, she is sick," he said. "And her financial situation is desperate."

"You put her in touch with the proper agencies?"

He shook his head. "She wouldn't hear of it. Said she'd starve before asking for charity."

"She'd let her children starve with her," Matt said, appalled by the very idea.

"No...she is feeding, taking care of the kids. She's just not taking care of herself."

"Her husband?"

He sighed. "Skipped out on her." A sad smile shadowed his lips. "She's not well disposed toward men at the moment...which is why I wanted to talk to you. I thought that perhaps if another woman spoke to her, explained that there was no shame in accepting help—" He broke off, frowning.

"You want me to stop by as a professional, explain to her—"

"No." David cut in with a quick shake of his head. "I feel the uniform might panic her."

"But then...how..." She gave him a helpless look.

He took a breath, then charged ahead. "I thought if we went to see her together, maybe, between the two of us, we could reassure her, convince her to allow us to help her through this rough period."

She hesitated, wanting and willing to do whatever she could, yet... There had to be any number of women who were active church parishioners who would be glad to accompany him in a visit to the woman; Corine, for instance.

The mere thought of the blond woman's name, the memory of the longing look in her eyes following

David as he walked away on the night of the church supper, caused a twinge inside Matt.

Stirred to life, her memory expanded to the afternoon she had spent with David, in his house, in his arms, in his bed. A longing ache throbbed through her.

"I need your help, Matt."

Matt capitulated. He needed her.

"When?" The remote tone she contrived didn't even impress her.

"Tomorrow, if you're free, the circumstances are pretty dire."

"I'm free," she admitted. "What time?"

"Nine?" He raised a brow, and lowered his voice. "I could pick you up."

Matt hesitated once more, telling herself to play it safe by taking her own car.

"Matt?" His soft voice curled around her heart.

"I'll be ready."

Chapter 10

David explained to Matt about the woman's position in more detail during the drive to her house the following morning.

"Her name is April Henderson. Ever since her husband took off...apparently with another woman, she has been earning money by cleaning house for several women in the new development across the road. Do you know where I mean?"

Matt nodded. "Elm Tree Gardens."

"Yes." He sighed. "She has no transportation, and not only can she take her son with her, she can walk there. Of course, she's being paid under the table."

"The girl's in school?"

"Yes. Not this week, of course, with the schools closed until after the New Year. Mrs. Henderson told me—insisted—that she was doing fine, earning enough to get along, until she got sick. She calls it a cold, but I'm afraid it sounds like pneumonia."

"I gather she hasn't seen a doctor."

"No." He slanted a sad smile at her. "She said she can't afford it as, since she hasn't been able to work, the money's running out."

Sharp concern nagged at Matt. "We've got to convince her to let us help, David."

"I know." He turned off the road onto a short dirt drive.

Matt passed the property every working day, taking little note of it.

The house was small, one of many of the ranch houses thrown up at the end of World War II to accommodate the horde of servicemen returning from overseas.

The woman looked worse than she had that day in church; her eyes were hollow, her breathing harsh.

When she'd come to the door in response to David's knock, it was immediately apparent to Matt that she didn't want to let them in.

"Mrs. Henderson, I've brought a friend to meet you," David said, his voice gentle, reassuring. "She'd like to explain the assistance available to you."

Caution and alarm sprang into the woman's eyes.

But before she could refuse his offer, close the door
in their faces, Matt took over.

"I do understand how you might feel about accepting charity, Mrs. Henderson," she said in strong
yet calming tones. "I promise, I will not attempt to
pressure you into anything."

The woman hesitated a moment more, during
which she was convulsed by a racking cough. "I—
I..." she began, between gasps for breath, and then
she sighed and pulled the door open as she stepped
back. "All right, you can come in, but..."

"I promise," Matt repeated.

She shyly ushered them into the small living
room. It was spotlessly clean, the furniture old but
well cared for. A small artificial tree stood in one
corner, a few toys and a short stack of shirt boxes
on the floor beneath it.

Thinking that at least the kids had had Christmas,
Matt opened her mouth to offer greetings of the season. Before she could speak, a banging sound reverberated through the house from the kitchen. The
tired-looking woman gave them a faint, apologetic
smile.

"That's Andy," she explained with the limp wave
of a hand. "If you don't mind coming into the
kitchen...he wants his breakfast."

"Not at all," Matt assured her with a smile, motioning for the woman to lead the way. "Is there
anything I can do to help?"

"No." She shook her head. "He's having cereal. We can talk while he eats."

The toddler was seated in an old wooden highchair, happily banging a plastic baby cup on the tray. Spying his mother, he began to chant a demand.

"Pup-eats, pup-eats."

"Yes, love, Mom's getting it for you." Her eyes, her smile, revealed pure love as she gazed at the boy. She turned to go to the countertop next to the sink, on which sat a box of cereal. Lifting the box, she shifted a wry look at Matt and David. "He loves puffed wheat," she said to interpret his demand. "Have a seat, this will only take a minute," she said, indicating the chairs neatly placed around the table.

After giving Andy his breakfast, the woman sat down across the table from Matt. "I better warn you," she said, her voice soft but decisive, "my parents were poor, but proud people. They never asked anyone for anything." Her voice grew firmer. "I won't go on welfare—my daddy would leave his grave and haunt me."

"All right." Matt accepted the woman's position without question. "But there are other organizations, church groups—" she indicated the silent man at the end of the table "—like Reverend Macdonough's, ready and willing to help in any way they can."

In a calm, steady voice, Matt spoke for some minutes, outlining the options available for those in temporary need of assistance.

"I'll be fine as soon as I can get back to work," the woman insisted, twisting the hands she'd folded on top of the table.

"You need to see a doctor," Matt said.

"I can't afford it." Her eyes burned with inner fever. "An office visit costs the earth these days."

"We'll take care of it." David spoke up for the first time. "Let us help you."

"I—I don't know. My daddy...I gotta think about it." Her movements jerky, she pushed her chair back and stood up. "I gotta call Jenny to eat." Casting a harried look at them, she rushed from the room.

With a sinking certainty that the woman was going to refuse their offer, Matt turned to stare at David in helpless despair of failure.

"David, I..."

"Pup-eats, pup-eats," Andy shouted, banging his empty bowl on the highchair tray.

Her mouth curving into an indulgent smile, Matt rose to accommodate him. "Hungry little tyrant, aren't you, big boy?" she said, laughing as he thrust the bowl at her. She had refilled the bowl with the cereal and milk and was placing it on the tray when his mother came running back into the room.

"She's gone...Jenny's gone," she cried, fear making her cold-roughened voice shrill.

David shot out of his chair. "What do you mean, she's gone?"

"She's not in the bedroom." Her head swiveled,

as if hoping to see the girl materialize in front of her wild, wide-eyed gaze. "She's nowhere in the house." Her searching gaze came to rest on Andy; a sob erupted from her throat. "I've got to get him dressed. We've got to look for Jenny, find her!"

"Calm down," Matt said with gentle authority, automatically taking control. "You are not well, and it's very cold outside. David and I will look for Jenny. You stay here, indoors, with Andy."

"But…but…" the woman began in protest.

"Mrs. Henderson," David broke in, "I think now is the time to tell you that Matt here is a policewoman with the Sprucewood Police Department."

If anything, rather than reassuring her, the information seemed to instill sheer panic. "Police!" she exclaimed. Her eyes flew to Matt. "Are you going to report me for not paying income taxes?"

"No," Matt said sharply. Then, more softly, "No, I am not going to report you, I'm going to help you."

The woman stared at Matt for a moment, then, apparently satisfied with what she gleaned from Matt's expression, she started to cry. "Please, please," she begged, sobbing. "Find Jenny for me. I—I couldn't bear it if anything happened to her."

"I'll do my best," Matt said, taking the woman's hand and giving it a comforting squeeze. "I promise."

* * *

"I'm going to report this." Matt's voice was tired. Her body was tired. Her mind was in rebellion.

"I know." David sounded every bit as tired as Matt.

It was dark, past dinnertime. They had spent the entire day searching for the missing girl. They had combed the immediate area around her home, the streets of Sprucewood and the surrounding communities. Checking off the names of Jenny's friends and school mates on the list her mother had given them, they had talked to the girls' friends, their parents, Jenny's teacher, all without success. The child seemed to have vanished.

"Are you thinking that maybe her father—"

"Yes," Matt interrupted him, anger, frustration and a niggling fear making her voice harsh. "Her father...or another sick someone who... Dammit," she exploded, too aware of the possibilities.

"We have to contact Mrs. Henderson again, explain what has to be done," he said, his tone reflecting the anger and fear in Matt's.

They had been calling the woman periodically throughout the day, each time hoping the girl had returned home on her own. She hadn't.

"We'd better find a phone, it'll be faster than running back into the station."

"We'll go to my place," David said. "It's closer than any pay phone I know of."

Matt was quiet as he turned the car, heading back

in the direction of his house. She raked her mind for
something she might have overlooked, some place
the child might have gone. She came up blank.

Sighing, she gazed through the windshield, staring
at the familiar tree-dotted landscape lining the road
leading to the driveway to the church.

Something, some movement, caught her eye as
David approached the turnoff.

"Slow down," she said, her voice low, sharp, as
she reached out to grasp his arm.

"Matt...what..." The car swerved, but David
controlled it, slowed it to a crawl. "What is it?"

"I see something—or someone. A shape, little
more than a shadow in the moonlight, moving
through the trees—" She broke off to point.
"There."

"I see," David said, his voice terse, tense. "A
person...a small person, heading toward the
church."

"Pull over," she ordered. "I'm going to follow
on foot."

"*We're* going to follow," he corrected her, pulling the car onto the shoulder and bringing it to a
stop.

She was out of the car like a shot.

He was right beside her.

Slowly, quietly, stealthily, they moved through the
wooded area, alert for any sign, any sound. There

was nothing but the rustle of the breeze through the stark, naked branches.

They were nearing the trees bordering the clearing around the church when they heard it...the unmistakable sound of a child weeping.

Matt and David came to a halt beside the large evergreen. They exchanged looks of confusion and consternation at the sight that met their startled eyes.

The girl was at the crèche, kneeling beside the cradle, sobbing her heart out. In the moonlight-bathed clearing, Matt could easily identify the child as Jenny.

"What in the world?" David breathed.

Matt shook her head, then raised a silencing finger to her lips. She moved noiselessly toward the scene. David stepped just as silently alongside her. As they drew nearer, they could hear, and understand, the girl's pleading confession.

"...And I'm sorry I hurt Your mother... but...but, I prayed, so hard, to Her to help my mommy. But she didn't. And my mommy got sicker and...and sicker...and I got scared and angry...and I thought...I thought, if she can't see my mommy...see how sick she was...then...then no one should be able to see Your mother, either. I took the can of paint my daddy used to cover the dents he got in the car when he was drunk and I...and I sprayed it to hide Your mother's face. But they fixed it so I covered her up with a trash bag...."

She sniffled. "And...and then, just yesterday, on Your birthday, that nice minister from the church came to see Mommy, came to help her. And...oh, little Baby Jesus...now I think it was Your mother that sent the minister to my mommy. I feel so bad about what I did...I...was so ashamed, I ran away to hide. I hid in that old barn down the road forever. I had to come...I had to tell You...I love You so...and I'm so sorry...." Jenny's voice dissolved in her heart-wrenching sobs.

Deeply affected, Matt turned a tear-blurred gaze on David. Her soul melted, her resistance surrendered to the love and compassion glowing from the depths of his eyes.

She loved this wonderful man, Matt acknowledged. She loved him. All other concerns were secondary.

Wiping the back of her hand across her eyes, she stepped into the clearing to go to the girl. As before, David was right beside her. Matt prayed he would always be beside her.

Jenny screamed in fright when Matt laid a gentle hand on her shoulder.

"It's all right, Jenny," she said in soft, crooning tones. "It's all right, now."

The girl turned wide, tear-bright eyes up at Matt. "Am I going to jail for what I did?" she cried, her thin frame shaking with fear and sobs.

"No, Jenny," David answered, kneeling next to the girl. "You're going home...to your mommy."

Chapter 11

"Case closed." Matt smiled at David over the rim of her coffee cup.

"There'll be no problems with this at the station?" He asked, concern tingeing his smile.

Matt shook her head. "Not unless you press charges." She arched a brow. "Are you?"

He gave her a look that drew a laugh from her, the first in what seemed a very long time.

"Everything has resolved itself very well, all things considered," he said, rising to go for the coffeepot to refill their cups.

"Hmm." Matt nodded, musing on the events following their discovery of the girl at the crèche.

April Henderson had been tearfully overjoyed

when Matt and David had arrived at the house, Jenny in tow. After hearing her daughter's story, and receiving Matt's word that she would handle the police matter, the woman broke down into sobs.

She also finally agreed to allow David and Matt to not only arrange a medical examination for her, but to set the wheels into motion for her to receive some assistance.

They had subsequently decided to get on it first thing in the morning. From the Henderson house, David had driven straight to his place.

Matt had been well aware of his purpose. At least, now, with her self-acknowledgment of her love for him, and her altered feelings about a relationship with him, she hoped she knew his purpose.

"I'd be a very happy man if my other problem, my primary problem, could be so satisfactorily resolved," David murmured, startling her out of her reverie.

He was standing next to her, the coffeepot forgotten in his hand. He stared down at her with blatant hunger in his eyes.

"What...problem is that?" she asked.

"You. Your lack of trust and faith in me. Your willingness to deny us both out of fear." He took a ragged breath and glanced at the coffeepot as if wondering how it had appeared in his hand. He slammed it onto the table with such force Matt was amazed it didn't shatter. Grasping her shoulders, he pulled her from the chair and into his arms, crushing her mouth with his.

His kiss seared her lips, stirred her soul, branded her his forever. Maybe the cop and the pastor could be a happening thing, after all.

"Dammit, Matt," David exploded when he raised his head. "I love you. Doesn't that mean anything to you?"

"It means everything to me," Matt said, her voice tight, thick with emotion, her heart full. "You mean everything to me."

He went rock still, staring into her eyes, hope flaring to life in his. "Are you saying what I'm almost afraid to believe you're saying?"

Matt smiled, flashing perfect white teeth.

"I'm saying," she said distinctly, "I love you. I'm saying my love for you is stronger than fear. I'm saying my faith in you is boundless. And I'm saying that I would trust you with my life."

David closed his eyes a moment. When he opened them again, the devilish gleam was back.

"I did warn you that I was stronger," he teased. "Didn't I?"

"Oh, my love, I wouldn't go that far." Suppressing a laugh, she gave him her assume-the-position look.

"How far would you go?" His eyes, those gorgeous blue eyes, danced with deviltry. "The bedroom?"

Matt lost control of her laughter. Pulling his head to hers, she kissed him, fast and hard. Then she placed her hand confidently in his.

"Lead on, Macdonough," she invited, excitement bubbling through her.

He didn't hesitate. Grasping her hand, he started for his bedroom.

"David, wait." Matt brought him up short with a sharp tug on his arm.

He groaned and closed his eyes. "Why?" His voice was ragged-edged with suppressed emotion.

"I...must call home."

His eyes flew open. "Call home? Matt..." he actually wailed before his voiced dwindled off, his expression revealing his confusion.

She gave him a helpless look and a hopeful smile. "They'll worry if it gets late and they don't hear from me. Not only Gram, but Lisa and my mother and..." She winced. "And my father."

"Uhh...huhh. Right. Your father. FBI. Big. Tough-looking. Not to mention your uncles... All big. All tough-looking. All law enforcement." He nodded. "Get on that phone, Matt."

Matt didn't even try to contain the laughter that bubbled into her throat. He sounded so intimidated...and looked so sexually frustrated. While she could believe the latter, the former was a joke.

As if David Macdonough could possibly be intimidated by her father or uncles. Her David, who had defeated his own personal Goliath.

Not in this lifetime.

The attack of giggles poured forth, rocketing through the kitchen.

And then, as quickly as Matt's laughter had begun, the giggles ceased, cut off by a sudden, startling, self-revelation.

Without conscious thought, she apparently had also defeated her own inner giant of trepidation—that of her determination against burdening a life partner with the fear and anxiety consistent with her profession.

David was frowning at her. "What?"

"I'm free." Matt heard the note of wonder in her voice, so wasn't surprised when his frown darkened.

"Excuse me?"

"I'll explain later," she said airily, turning to stroll to the wall phone. "Right now, I'm going to call Gram." She lifted the receiver, then paused, a smile curling her lips. "On second thought, I think I'll ask to speak to Mother…" She tossed him a grin. "She's been there, she'll understand."

"I wish I did."

Matt heard his muttered comment over the sound of the phone ringing in her grandmother's house.

"Wolfe residence," Lisa answered.

"Hi, Lis, it's me. May I speak to Mom?"

"Sure…but where in the world have you been all

day?'' Lisa didn't wait for a response, but went on dryly, "Fooling around with the reverend, are you?''

"Actually, I was working,'' Matt returned, every bit as dryly. "We were both working...in fact, we solved a case of church desecration.''

"Oh. I see.'' Lisa sounded so disappointed, Matt had to smile. "Well, then, congratulations.''

"Thanks.'' Her amusement overflowed into her voice. "Now, may I speak to Mom?''

"Yes, of course. Hold on.''

There were a few moments of murmurs in the background at the other end of the line, during which Matt slid a quick sparkling glance at David.

He sparkled back at her; only his sparkle contained more sensuousness than amusement.

Matt felt tiny pinpricks of excitement over every inch of her skin...and deeper. She took in a long, calming breath; it didn't help.

"Matt?''

She blinked at the smooth, serene sound of her mother's voice. "Oh...hi, Mom.'' Matt scowled at her own inanity.

"Hi, yourself,'' Sandra said in her natural unruffled manner. "You wanted to talk to me?'' A gentle but determined maternal nudge.

"Yes, yes...er...'' Matt wet her lips, took another deep breath, reminded herself that she was a mature, intelligent professional, then rushed into garbled speech. "I probably won't be home until late...so...

ah, don't you, Gram, or any one of you wait up. I'm
with David, and…I, er, well, we…"

"Matilda." Sandra's soft tone sliced through her
daughter's incoherent explanation.

Matt sighed in self-despair. "Yes, Mother?"

"Are you trying to tell me—in your own inimi-
table way—that you and that most attractive man
have a *thing* in the bud between you?"

Matt exhaled in relief. She really should have remembered that her mother was one very shrewd,
very savvy lady.

"Yes, Mother, that is precisely what I'm trying to
tell you," Matt answered with blunt candor.

"And could this *thing* evolve into something serious?" Sandra probed further.

Matt shot a quick look at David…and stopped
breathing altogether for a moment. The sparkle was
gone from his eyes. Those incredible blue eyes were
staring at her with an open expression of adoration.

"Oh…I strongly suspect it could, Mother," Matt
said, brilliantly illuminated to the depths of her being
by the light of love for her glowing in David's eyes.

"I see. In that case, my blessing upon you both.
And don't worry, no one will wait up."

"What about Dad?" she asked, well aware of her
father's overprotective tendency toward his daughters.

"Don't worry about him, either." Sandra's laugh
was soft. "I can handle your father."

Matt could attest to that. She was still smiling moments later when she hung up the receiver.

"What about your father?" David asked, concerned. "Is there a problem?"

She turned, her smile easy, her eyes reflecting the light of love back to him. "No, no problem," she said, extending her hand to him again.

Though he captured her hand with his, he hesitated. "But, I heard you say…"

She silenced him with a quick headshake. "Not to worry, Mother will take care of Dad."

"I like your mother." The deviltry was back in his eyes.

"And she approves of you." Needing no urging, she strolled beside him from the kitchen, along the hallway, and into his bedroom.

"I like your father, too." David halted beside his bed and pulled her into his arms. "And I like your grandmother, your sister, your aunts, uncles and cousins."

"I'm glad." She chuckled and curled her arms around his neck. "And, from their response to you last night, I know they like you, too. Now…"

Matt lowered her voice to a sexy murmur, "Can we forget about the family…and concentrate on us?"

He smiled and lowered his head to brush her lips with his. "I was afraid you'd never—"

His voice got lost inside her mouth.

His kiss was passionate, possessive, all-consuming. Matt reveled in it, gloried in it, returned it with every cell and molecule in her body.

It was still the Christmas holiday season, but for Matt, it might as well have been the Fourth of July. She saw the rockets' red glares, felt the bombs bursting, and surrendered to the sheer delight of it…of David.

She tugged at his shirt buttons with eager, trembling fingers. He caught her hand in his.

"Slowly," he murmured against her kiss-sensitized lips. "I want to savor the moment, savor you."

Aroused and anxious, Matt pulled her head back to gaze at him in frustration. "But…but…" she protested. "I want to touch you, David."

The expression that skittered across his face was one of unabashed joy. "Oh, my beautiful Matt, you can't begin to imagine how much I want you to touch me. And I want to touch you, touch you and kiss you, every inch of you." Raising a hand, he drew a finger down her cheek—which drew a longing sigh from her. "But slowly, my love. Let me show you how much you mean to me."

As before, he began with her hair, freeing the confined mass by removing the large butterfly clip anchoring the loose twist at the back of her head. The long, deeply waved strands tumbled onto her shoulders and into his hands.

"I love your hair. It's like autumn-burnished gold silk," he murmured, spearing his fingers into the tresses to pull her mouth to his.

This time his kiss was different. Applying the lightest pressure, he claimed her mouth with heart-wrenching care and gentleness.

Her senses seduced, Matt sighed and melted against the solid strength of his body.

With exquisite tenderness, David slowly removed her clothes, caressing her skin with featherlight strokes as each separate piece fell away.

His touch was so very tender, loving, Matt felt both cherished and adored. She was quivering in response by the time she at last stood naked and unashamed before him in readiness.

Her hands moved once again to the buttons on his shirt; this time David did not stop her. Past subtlety, she divested him of his garments within minutes.

When the last item was gone, Matt smoothed her hands over his shoulders, his chest. Her palms tingled from the friction of the wedge of dark hair against her skin. Her senses whirled in response to the strength of the trim, angular, muscled length of him, her body quickening to the allure of his musky aroused-male scent.

Groaning low in his throat, David pulled her into his arms, letting her feel the power of his need.

They sank as one onto the bed. Matt arched into him in silent supplication.

''No, love. Not yet. Not yet,'' he whispered, gliding his tongue over her lips.

Matt made a low throaty sound of protest when he abandoned her mouth, then sighed as his lips commenced a journey down the arch of her neck. He paused to nip and lave at the curve of her shoulder before stringing quick, stinging kisses down her chest.

Matt bowed her spine.

David accepted her invitation to explore the rounded curves of her breasts. She cried out when at last, at last, he closed his lips around one taut, aching tip, and shuddered in response when he began to suckle.

He lavished his attention on her breasts for long, sense-whirling minutes, then abandoned them to continue his exploration. With his lips and tongue and warm breath setting her body on fire, he touched her everywhere, *everywhere,* making her frantic with need.

Her breath reduced to ragged gasps, Matt tangled her fingers in his hair, writhing beneath his erotic assault on her senses. Anticipation, excitement and tension spun wildly, on the very edges of control.

''David...please,'' she pleaded, tugging frantically on his hair. ''I—I...can't bear any more.''

''Yes...now,'' he said, his voice tight, strangled, as he surged up and over her. ''Now.''

Matt was beyond thinking, beyond noticing, beyond caring that there were no moments spent fumbling with foil-wrapped packages. Her desire to be joined with him, be one with him, had reached flash point.

With a whimper of relief when finally he was inside her, she encircled his muscle-bunched flanks within the lover's embrace of her thighs.

David, the tendons rigid in his arched neck, did his best to control the pace, stretching it out to the nth of delicious pleasure.

But he had prepared Matt too well. Hungry, needful, she drove him on, to the very end of his tether, and with a groan of defeat, he gave in to the moment.

From there, their ride was wild, exhilarating; but it was short-lived.

Matt's outcry of ecstasy was followed within seconds by David's shuddering exclamation of completion.

It was late. Matt was lost to the world in slumber, her burnished gold hair a glorious drift of silk across the pillow.

Disentangling himself from her, Mac silently slipped from the bed.

She murmured a protest.

He froze.

The breath he was holding eased from his throat when she snuggled deeper into the covers, deeper into sleep. Then, naked as the day he came into the world, he walked to the window to stare out and up into the star-tossed, moon-bright sky.

Your servant, Sir, he addressed his ultimate Commander. *Just as I am…as the old hymn goes.*

I love her, as You surely know, love her so much, so very much, it's almost frightening. And, yes, Sir, I am afraid. I'm afraid to sleep, to close my eyes, for fear of waking up to find her gone again. I know…I know, it's unreasonable and precipitate, but I don't ever again want to wake up alone and without her.

I've been alone so long, as You also surely know. And I've waited so long…not even knowing what or who I was waiting for. But You knew, didn't You?

Did You choose her for me at the beginning?

Have I served well enough to deserve her love, her trust, her faith?

She, my beautiful Officer Wolfe, is a dedicated warrior in the battle between right and wrong. She is a woman with many strengths, purpose, principle. Whereas I, as only You know, have struggled against many weaknesses.

And yet, Sir, this most adored woman has declared her love for me.

I pray I prove worthy of the bounty and the blessing…Yours and hers…

A sensation woke Matt, a strange sensation of feeling bereft and alone. But that's silly, she thought, her mind still sleep-muzzy. She had slept alone all her life. Why would she now feel cold, alone and deserted?

David.

That quick, Matt was awake and alert. David was no longer with her, his body spooned to hers.

For an instant, panic flared…

Matt pushed herself up on one forearm and skimmed her gaze around the room. Her gaze came to rest on the naked solitary figure outlined against the window. Her sigh of relief whispered into the still night.

Leaving the warmth of the bed, the carpet silencing her movements, she went to him.

"David," she murmured, lifting a hand, yet hesitating to touch his motionless form. "What are you doing?"

He didn't hesitate for an instant. His stare remaining fixed on the sky, he reached out, curling an arm around her waist, pulling her to his side, to his chilled body.

"I was praying," he answered simply.

Praying? Matt cast a glance at the sky, embarrassment heating her cheeks. He—they—were standing at the window, naked and exposed before the twinkling eyes scattered across the night sky.

And the all-seeing eyes of their Creator.

She made a strangled sound of despair.

"What is it?" David shifted his stare to her, concern sharp in his voice. "What's wrong?"

"You're praying?" she whispered, finding it oddly difficult to drag her eyes from the sky. "Like this?" A sweep of her hand indicated their nudity.

He chuckled. "My sweet Officer Wolfe, do you honestly think it matters?"

Matt sent a fast, uneasy glance to the night sky. "Isn't it...well...disrespectful?"

His chuckle grew into a full-fledged laugh. "Oh, Matt," he murmured, the residue of laughter woven through his voice. "You must realize that layers and layers of the heaviest clothing could not conceal the most infinitesimal flaw, physical or mental, from His notice."

"I suppose," she conceded, although still not quite comfortable.

"The unadorned human form is His design," he reminded her, his arm tightening to pull her even closer, so close, she could feel the tiny goose bumps on his flesh.

"Yes, you're right," she agreed, though still uncertain.

He chuckled again.

Matt decided to change the subject.

"What were you praying for?" she asked, snuggling closer, trying to warm him with her own body.

"Guidance." Again his answer was simple, to the point, his gaze returning to the star-bright sky.

"In what?" She looked up at him, loving the strength of his rough-hewn features, the devotion reflected in his eyes; loving him, the wonderful man that was David.

"All things…generally." Canting his head, he smiled at her. "But right now…you in particular."

"Me?" She frowned, feeling a twinge of unease. "I—I don't understand. Why would you seek—need—guidance for me in particular?"

"How to proceed." Again, a simple statement.

"David…really, you're going to have to do better than that," she protested. "Proceed with what?"

"With you."

"But…I don't know—" she began when, yet again, he didn't elaborate.

"No," he interrupted her. "Before I explain, I must ask you something. What did you mean earlier, when you said you were free? Free of what? To do what?"

"Free of the misguided resolve I'd made to never subject a man to the uncertainty and anxiety of being the mate of a law enforcement officer," she confessed, gazing up into his beloved face with her feelings for him as bared to his eyes as her nakedness. "Free to love you."

He seemed not to breathe for a moment, and when he did, it was shallow, uneven. "I can be trusted with your love, Matt. Please believe that."

She would have answered, but he went on.

"I will be anxious, uncertain, and flat-out scared when you are working. But I'll endure. I'll be waiting for you when you return to me. I will pray and keep the faith."

"I know that...now," she said. "And I will keep faith with you. Trusting you. Loving you."

David exhaled a heartfelt sigh. Then he swung his gaze back to the sky.

"Thank You, Sir."

Matt heard his barely audible murmur, felt the tremor of easing tension ripple through his body. So simple a thank you...and so very complex.

"David?" Her throat felt tight; her eyes felt the sting of tears.

"Yes, love?" His voice, so gentle, so tender, so very loving in tone, sent the tears over the barriers of her eyelids.

"You feel so cold...come back to bed." She moved to turn away; his other arm encircled her, held her still against his chilled form.

"I'm afraid."

She blinked. "Of what?"

"Of falling asleep." His lips curved in a self-deprecating smile. "And then waking later to find you have crept away from me again."

"I won't." Raising a hand, she touched fingertips to his cool cheek, his firm lips. "I'll sleep beside you through the night. I promise."

"Your family." He sighed. "Your father."

Yes, her family. Her father. Matt knew she had a tough decision to make; she made it in an instant.

"I love, respect and honor my family…most especially my father," she said, shivering as his cold pervaded her dwindling warmth. "But I have made my choice, David. From now on, my place is by your side," she vowed. "Wherever you may be."

"And if I should receive a call, be transferred?" he asked. "It happens in the ministry, you know."

"I love my work, David."

"I know."

"I love you more." Rising up, she kissed his mouth. "And I will never ask you to choose between me and your commitment to your faith."

"You'd go with me…" David's voice cracked with emotion. "Just like that?"

"Just try and get away from me." She gave him a tear-sparkled, teasing look. "I'm a trained police officer, if you'll recall?"

"Yeah." Laughter shimmered in his voice. "So?"

"I'll follow you, find you, imprison you. Never let you go."

"It's a deal." The laughter escaping, David swept her up into his arms and carried her to the bed.

Laughing with him, Matt pulled him down with her when he lowered her to the cover-strewn mattress.

In scant seconds, desire chased the chill from her body.

Matt was content with the heat David generated within her. She was hoping for a long, cold winter.

* * * * *

WOLFE WONDER

To Melissa and Tara:
Thanks, guys, for your faith.

Chapter 1

It was starting to snow, and it wasn't kidding around. The lacy white stuff swirled and danced on the wind.

"Oh, great," Lisa Wolfe muttered, activating the wipers to clear the large splattering flakes from the windshield. "*Now* it snows, *now* that the holidays are over."

Fortunately, at nine forty-five on a Monday morning, with the school bus and auto rush over, traffic on the Schuylkill Expressway was fairly light. Not that traffic or snow bothered Lisa all that much; having lived her whole life in Denver, Colorado, she was used to both conditions.

But presently, Lisa wasn't in Colorado, she was

in her brother-in-law's four-wheel-drive SUV in Pennsylvania, had been in the state since a few days before Christmas. It hadn't flurried a flake until now.

Lisa had been visiting her sister, grandmother and assorted aunts, uncles and cousins. Her parents had been with her; Lisa had seen them off on a flight to Denver some thirty minutes ago. They had enjoyed a wonderful—if snowless—Christmas and New Year's celebration with the Wolfe pack...as her father referred to his mostly male family members.

Keeping her gaze firmly on the road and the sparse traffic around her, Lisa recalled the previous two weeks; the warmth and abundance of laughter, chatter...family—a lot of family—and every one talking at once. That is, when they weren't fussing over Lisa's twin sister, Matt.

Matt. A stupid nickname for a young woman. Lisa sighed and smiled at the same time. Her sister had been named for their father's mother, Matilda, whom everyone called Maddy. Their mother, Sandra, having bestowed the name on her first-born—by five minutes—daughter, had emphatically made it known that there was no way she would call her by it. The consensus had then been that it would be too confusing to have two Maddys in the family. After much discussion, time out for eating, laughing and teasing, along with the usual uproar amongst the family members present at that time, Lisa's father, Cameron, had come up with Matt.

The nickname seemed to fit, and so Lisa's twin, the poor dear, was stuck with the male sobriquet.

Closing the gates to memory, Lisa concentrated on exiting the expressway onto highway 422. The snow, coming down harder now, had already laid a coating on the ground. She gently depressed the brake pedal, testing the condition of the roadway.

Good. Lisa sighed, releasing the tightness in muscles she hadn't realized she had tensed. The brakes gripped. No fishtailing, no slipping, no sliding; PennDOT was on the job, keeping the highways treated and as clear as possible for the motorists.

Fully aware that she was about half an hour—give or take, considering weather conditions—from her destination of Sprucewood, Lisa, mindful of her driving, allowed more recent memories to resume unwinding inside her head.

Matt. Lisa smiled as she reviewed her earlier thoughts of the family fussing over her sister, her pregnant-with-twins sister.

Fussing? Over Matt?

As if. The very idea elicited a chuckle. Oh, they all had tried to fuss, most especially Sandra and Cameron, the grandparents-to-be.

Matt was having none of it. Lisa laughed aloud as the exasperated sound of Matt's voice replayed in her mind.

Now, look, you guys, I don't have to be babied, coddled or anything like that, she had said in her strongest tone, the one she had used as a Sprucewood cop when dealing with particularly hard-assed criminals. Sweeping a stern look over assembled family members, she had declared, *I'm not ill, for heaven's sake, I'm pregnant.*

And big as a house with the twins, Lisa had thought at the time, suppressing a grin.

While I do appreciate the caring intentions, I assure you, one and all, that I am fine. Matt had brought her sweeping glance to a stop on her husband. A soft smile had curved her lips. *David takes very good care of me.*

David being Matt's husband, the Reverend David Macdonough, called Mac by family, friends and just about everybody else. Matt and Mac. Lisa laughed aloud. Personally, she thought it was a hoot. Like her sister, Lisa preferred to call her brother-in-law by his given name, David.

I do my best, David had responded, his eyes soft with the glow of love for his wife. *But, since I've had to be out of the house pretty much lately, busy with my pastoral duties, and community work, I'm glad and thankful Lisa will be staying with us until after the babies come.*

Well, so am I, Matt had agreed, tossing a wide smile at Lisa. *Not because I need taking care of or fussing over, but because it'll be fun. It's been so long since she and I have spent quality time together, had some long gabfests, and I've missed our "girl talks."*

Too true. It had been a long time. She had missed their gabfests and shared laughter as well, Lisa thought now, nearly two weeks later. It had been much too long since they had shared secrets and giggles. Although nice, long-distance phone calls were simply not the same. Besides, since their shortest call *ever* had still run close to an hour, the cost, however worth it, was pretty impressive.

Until now—although there had been a lot of laughter and conversation, usually with everyone talking at once—she and Matt still hadn't had a chance for a long, cozy chat; it hadn't remained quiet long enough.

With the holidays over, their parents headed back to Colorado and aunts, uncles and cousins returning to their own homes in different sections of the country, things would settle down now. They'd probably be too quiet for a while, Lisa reflected, taking the exit off 422 onto the road that would take her to Sprucewood.

Too quiet? After the previous couple of weeks? Had she said bye-bye to her senses? Lisa grinned at her reflection as she checked the rearview mirror.

Of course, not all of the family members had scattered. Their grandmother, the original Matilda, lived in Sprucewood, in the same house she and Lisa's late grandfather had moved into soon after their marriage. They had raised their four sons there. Lisa's father, Cameron, was the eldest, followed by Royce, Eric and Jake—the only one who still lived in Sprucewood. He was now the Chief of Police and had been Matt's superior when she was a patrol officer on the force.

Lisa chuckled again at the thought. In one form or another, nearly all of her family members were in law enforcement. Her father had gone into the FBI after finishing law school. Her three uncles were cops: Royce with the Pennsylvania State Police, Eric in the narcotics unit of the Philadelphia Police Force and, of course, Jake, the chief right here in Sprucewood.

Practically all of her cousins, every one of them male, were in law enforcement, from city police to highway patrol, border patrol and even one Marine Corps MP.

There was one exception. Her Uncle Jake and Aunt Sarah's youngest son, Tanner, was the rebel. Like his father many years before him, Tanner made his own rules, went his own way. The family saw him only on rare occasions. Jake had dubbed Tanner the Wandering Wolfe. Lisa and her mother, of course, were lawyers.

Lisa's cousins and their wives had produced a few, three to be exact, female offspring. It was too early to tell if any of the young girls would go into some form of law enforcement, but, so far, none of them appeared inclined in that direction. Maybe because they were still little more than toddlers.

Thinking of the youngsters reminded Lisa that there would soon be two more added to the family mix. Another set of twins. Lisa laughed. Who would have thought? Hadn't they always heard that twins skipped a generation?

Matt and Mac...Lisa shook her head. Matt and Mac, indeed. Anyway, her sister and brother-in-law didn't know the sex, or sexes, of the babies. The doctor knew from the ultrasound, but Matt and David didn't want to know beforehand. They wanted to find out when the babies arrived.

And that event wouldn't be too far from now, Lisa reminded herself, thrilling to the very thought. Matt's due date was early March, but the doctor thought it unlikely that she would go full-term.

From the sheer size of her uncomfortable-looking sister, Lisa was inclined to agree with the doctor. Coming out of her reverie, Lisa caught herself just in time before she drove right by the driveway leading to David's church and the rectory a short distance beyond.

The church was beautiful with the snow whirling around it. While not yet ten years old, it had a stately, old-world look, like a church positioned near a castle nestled in the valley of a mountain range in some faraway country.

Lisa shook her head, dissolving the romantic

scene as she carefully maneuvered the curving inclined driveway past the church building. She brought the vehicle to a smooth stop in front of Matt and David's house.

Having been given free run of the place, Lisa didn't bother to knock. After stamping the snow from her boots—not snow boots, but very expensive knee-high, high-heeled leather dress boots, worn under a riding-style long skirt—she opened the door and stepped into the welcoming warmth of her sister's cozy living room.

The room was empty. Hearing voices from the back of the house, she hung her ankle-length coat in the hall closet, then made her way past the dining room and along the hallway to the kitchen. She came to a halt in the doorway upon sight of a stranger seated at the glass-topped table opposite Matt and David. The trio were bent over what looked like blueprints spread out on the table. The stranger had a lustrous mass of thick, deeply waved black hair, with just a touch of silver streaking his temples.

"Hi," Lisa cheerily announced herself. "Anybody home?"

Boing. Boing. Boing. Three heads popped up.

"Oh, hi, Lis," Matt said, heaving a relieved sigh. "I'm glad you're home safe. I was getting worried. What kind of condition are the roads in?"

"Not too bad, the road crews are on the job, and

so far, on top of the situation," Lisa replied, sliding a frankly curious look at the stranger.

"I told you she'd be okay, she's used to this kind of weather," David said, smiling at her. "Hi, Lis. Come on in, I want you to meet someone."

Sliding back his chair, the stranger stood up...and up...way, way up.

Lisa felt a sudden sinking sensation, and a strange something that felt like a hot wire sizzle through her body from her head to her toes.

Weird.

David was a tall, very attractive man, with a hard-lived roughness etched into his features, the harshness relieved by the soft light of compassion in his eyes.

The man now standing was a good two inches taller than David, and some six inches taller than she and Matt, which put him at about an imposing height of six foot five or six.

And he was completely, absolutely, no-doubt-about-it, steal-your-breath gorgeous...in a thoroughly masculine way. He also was completely masculine in build. He had a long, lean-muscled body that just wouldn't quit, with broad chest and shoulders, narrow waist and hips and long, straight legs.

Lisa was so bemused by the look of him, she nearly missed David's introduction.

"Lisa, this is Carrick Fitzhugh of Fitzhugh Builders. You remember, I told you he was building our new house?''

''Yes, of course.'' Lisa extended her hand, proud of the cool, in-control tone and manner she had managed. ''Nice to meet you, Mr. Fitzhugh.''

''The pleasure's mutual, and…''

''And Fitz, this is Lisa,'' David cut in, laughing. ''We all call her Lis.''

''And people call me Fitz,'' he said in a deep, honey-warm voice, taking her soft, slender hand into his much larger, work-roughened one. His hand was as warm as his voice.

Lisa felt a shiver dance a two-step up her spine, intensifying the sizzle still crackling inside her. She also felt slightly stunned, speechless…a shockingly new experience for her, considering her profession.

''You're the lawyer,'' Fitzhugh said, as if he had been monitoring her thoughts.

''Yes,'' Lisa murmured, feeling a twinge of regret when he released her hand.

''In your mother's law firm, I understand.''

Lisa's spine stiffened, bringing the tap dance to a jarring halt at her nape. The inner sizzle sputtered to an empty sensation. Had she detected a shade of condescension coloring his tone? What, precisely, did he think he understood? That she was the pampered and probably spoiled darling, playing lawyer in her mother's offices?

Lisa had encountered that attitude before, always

from men, when she had first joined forces with her mother. But it had been years...

"Yes." Though she bristled inside, wanting nothing so much as to take him apart verbally, cut him down to size, Lisa hung on, if barely, to her pleasant tone and manner. "I've been working with her since high school."

"And, from all reports, she's a regular tiger, a man eater, at that," David said in a teasing tone.

"Indeed? A man eater, humm?" One of Fitz's dark, winged eyebrows took flight. His voice held a sensual, suggestive hint. "How so?"

Lisa sucked in a soft hissing breath.

"Don't be crass, Fitz." Matt's frown of disapproval was belied by the humor edging her voice, lighting her eyes. "What David meant was, Lisa has the reputation of being one of, if not *the* best divorce lawyer in Denver...possibly in the entire state of Colorado. Men with marriage troubles, or those in danger of being caught being unfaithful, tremble at the mention of the name *Lisa Wolfe* on their wives' lips."

Lisa rolled her eyes. "Matilda, really."

"Uh-oh, now you've done it," David chided his wife. He grinned at Fitz. "Lis only ever calls Matt *Matilda* when she's about to lose her cool."

"Yeah," drawled the former police officer. "She scares the hell out of me when she calls me that."

"Sure, sure," Lisa drawled right back at her sister, still inwardly seething, but relieved and grateful for the change of subject, even if it was silly. "Big tough cop scared of her younger sister."

"I'm older only by five minutes," Matt shot back, beginning to laugh.

"Do these two Amazons go through this performance very often?" Fitz asked David in mild curiosity, glancing from one six-foot-tall woman to the other.

David nodded. "They love it. It's their way of having fun, and showing affection for each other. The whole family's like that. You should hear it when they're all together."

"As if this family has ever been all together," Lisa inserted dryly.

Matt laughed.

David grinned.

"The Wolfe pack you told me about?" Fitz asked, shifting an amused glance from one to the other.

"Yeah." David nodded again.

"Amazon," Matt finally managed to stop giggling to interject. She swept a slow, cool look the long length of Fitz's body. "Look who's talking."

"I'm not an Amazon," he corrected her in gentle, teasing tones. "Amazons are female."

No, Carrick Fitzhugh was not an Amazon, he was a near-giant, and decidedly male. Lisa kept the thought to herself, while again attempting to change the direction of the conversation—such as it was.

"Are those the blueprints for your house?" she asked, indicating the papers spread out on the table.

"Oh, yes," Matt said, pleasure and excitement lighting her eyes. "Wanna see?"

"Well, of course." Lisa moved closer to the table, but opposite Fitz. Though she had been to the building site the day after she and her parents had arrived, she really hadn't gotten a clear idea of what the house would look like. The workers were putting the finishing touches to the roof, but the inside was still little more than a shell of support beams and flooring boards. And it had been colder than a tomb.

Settling into a chair, Lisa's gaze skimmed the three cups anchoring the prints. "I'd love some coffee, too, if there's any left," she said coaxingly, slanting an imploring smile at her sister. "It's been over five hours since my last cup, when Mom and Dad and I had breakfast with Gramma." She sniffed, delicately. "And do I smell David's secret special-recipe chili simmering on the stove?"

"You do." Matt grinned. "He started cooking it first thing this morning, just for you."

"Hmmm, wonderful," Lisa murmured, flashing her killer smile at her brother-in-law. "Thank you, David."

Fitz uttered a sound, low in his throat, as if trying to catch his breath, then coughed.

"You're welcome." David shot a curious glance at Fitz. "You all right?"

"Fine," Fitz assured him. "I like chili," he offered the information, to anyone he hoped might be interested.

"I made some corn bread to go with the chili," Matt put in, smiling at Fitz.

Lisa groaned. "Be still my heart."

"I like corn bread, too."

David chuckled. "You wouldn't be angling for an invitation to lunch, would you, Fitz?"

Fitz gave him a wry look. "Groveling, actually."

Yeah, right, Lisa thought, smothering a burst of laughter; she couldn't picture Fitz groveling for anything, not even his life…never mind a meal of chili and corn bread. The very idea was absolutely ludicrous.

Laughing softly, as if she also found the idea of Fitz groveling ridiculous, Matt headed for the coffeemaker set on the countertop.

"Can I help?" Lisa asked, taking a step away from the table.

"No." Matt smiled at her. "You look over the plans with David and Fitz, Lisa. I'll brew some fresh coffee and bring you a cup, with a couple cookies, to hold you till lunch."

"I like cookies, too, Matt," Fitz offered the unsolicited information.

Lisa shook her head, setting a gold-tinged blond tendril loose from the previously neat twist at her nape.

David roared with laughter.

"Stop whining, Fitz," Matt ordered from the sink. "We're all having coffee and cookies."

"Now I ask you, was I whining?" Fitz was staring directly into Lisa's dark-brown eyes.

Lisa felt a jolt of *something* at the glitter of challenge in the depths of his piercing dark-blue eyes.

"Of course, you were," David chided Fitz, saving Lisa from trying to find her voice to respond. "But, then, who wouldn't whine for Maddy's cookies?"

Nobody Lisa could think of.

Within less than ten minutes, the heady aroma of steaming coffee and warmed cookies wafted to the table from the large tray in Matt's hands.

"Let me take that." The offer came in chorus from David and Fitz, who had both jumped up to help.

Well, at least Fitzhugh was capable of being a gentleman, or at any rate acting like one, Lisa mused, with a hefty dash of skepticism.

Within minutes, they were all sipping delicious spiced coffee and nibbling on her grandmother's scrumptious chewy chocolate-chip and pecan cookies, somehow left over from holiday entertaining. Lisa examined the blue line drawings of the two-and-a-half-story house under construction for Matt and David.

"Five bedrooms?" She asked in surprise, glancing from her sister to her brother-in-law.

"Sure. We're going to want more children," David answered, smiling softly at Matt, who nodded in agreement. His smile slid into a devilish grin as he turned back to Lisa. "And who knows, we might even have more twins."

Matt laughed.

"What do you suppose the odds are on that happening?" Fitz wondered aloud.

"A couple hundred to one?" David guessed.

"More than that," Lisa said, dismissively, returning her attention to the plans. Her eyebrows arched. "You're having in-law quarters attached?"

"They're already attached," Fitz clarified.

"For Gram, if she needs them," Matt said.

"You mean, if she'll come, whether she needs to or not." Lisa's voice was rueful. "Having lived with her until you married David, you know as well as—maybe more than anyone—how independent Gram is."

Matt nodded. "Yes, but I wanted her to have a place of her own, all on one floor, close to us, but private…in case she needs it."

Lisa smiled at Matt with gentle affection. "Of course, I understand and completely agree, but this place has to be costing a bundle. I haven't a clue what new homes are going for here in Pennsylvania, but I know the expense of a property this size," she indicated the blueprints, "would be exorbitant in Denver."

Before either Matt or David could respond, Fitz told her the bottom-line price, including the property lot and the house under construction on it.

It wasn't nearly as high as Lisa had expected, but it wasn't peanuts, either. She had an idea, and even though she felt certain of what Matt and David's response would be, she put the thought into words anyway.

"I'd like to help. May I write a check for you guys, for a late Christmas gift or early anniversary present?"

"That's very thoughtful, Lis, but..." David began, only to be interrupted by his wife.

"No, no," Matt shook her head, pushing her bulk out of her chair to go to Lisa to give her a hug. "I...we, appreciate the offer, it's so generous, and so like you." She kissed Lisa's cheek, sniffed and blinked the emotional mist from her eyes. "Like you, and like Mom and Dad and Gram, and even like Uncle Jake and Aunt Sarah."

"What?" Lisa managed to sound shocked and indignant, while hugging her sister back. "No offers at all from the other uncles and aunts?"

Matt sniffled again, then grinned. "No, but then, none of the others saw the house or the prints or heard the price. I mean, these last couple weeks have been wild, as you know, with all the uncles, aunts, cousins and their families. Who was thinking about house plans?"

Lisa laughed. "Mom, Dad, Gram, Jake and Sarah." Her smile slid into a mock frown. "Which begs the question. How come I haven't seen them until now?"

"Why, because," Matt grinned again, impish this time. "You were busy with Mom and Dad, Gram and all the…"

Laughing, Lisa held up her hands, silencing her teasing sister. "I got it. I got it."

"Is it contagious?" Fitz asked, with quiet and absolutely feigned innocence.

David chuckled.

Matt laughed.

"Very funny." Lisa spared Fitz a narrow-eyed glance that said just the opposite before returning her attention to the blueprints. For some reason she couldn't fathom, Carrick Fitzhugh rattled her on a personal, basic level.

"I do my best to amuse," he rejoined, drolly.

"How nice." There was an edge to her voice that Lisa couldn't conceal; hell, she didn't even try to conceal it. The man annoyed her. Strange.

"Lis?" Matt shot her a curious frown, as if to say, What's bugging you, anyway?

Lisa shrugged, but surrendered, reluctantly, to conventional manners. "I'm sorry…" she apologized, offering a weak smile as her gaze swept the three faces staring at her. "Maybe hunger is making me irritable."

"Or maybe the weather...or something," David said, a gleam of speculation in his eyes, shifting a look between Lisa and Carrick Fitzhugh.

"It's hunger," Lisa retorted.

Lowering her head in an unsuccessful bid to hide a slight smile, Matt began gathering the plans together. "Then let's put these away until later and get lunch on the table."

"You don't have to get them out again for me," Lisa said, getting up to help her sister. "I don't get a very good perspective from the plans. I'd much rather see the house, the progress that has been made since I saw it before Christmas."

"That's good," David said. "You can take over from Matt, as I'd prefer she didn't traipse back and forth anymore."

Lisa frowned at him. "Traipse back and forth? I don't understand."

Fitzhugh chuckled.

"Honestly." Matt heaved a long, loud sigh. "I've been making regular trips to watch the progress on the house. And Galahad here—" she waved at David "—wants me to stop going. He insists I'm getting too big to go *traipsing*."

"You are," Lisa agreed, laughing at Matt's frustrated expression. "Isn't the ground still uneven and bumpy, the way it was when Mom, Dad and I were there?"

"It is," Fitz asserted, with authority.

"And it'll get worse with a snow cover," David pointed out, deep concern in his voice. "You could fall."

"David," Matt objected. "I'll be fine."

"No." David adamantly shook his head.

"That settles it, then," Lisa announced. "I'll go."

"Every day," Matt said.

"Every day?" Lisa repeated, incredulously.

David sighed. "She's been going every day, very likely either to the workers' amusement, or their impatience with her incessant questions."

"But, why, for heaven's sake?"

"Well, because…" Matt began.

"Matt," Fitz cut in, his expression rigid, rock-hard. "Has someone said something to you about stopping by so often?" His tone was even harder than his expression.

Lisa suppressed a shiver.

"Oh, no," Matt exclaimed. "They have all been very polite and helpful."

"They'd better be."

The shiver inside Lisa intensified. Turning away from the sight of his harshly set features, she moved to the sink to get a dishcloth to wipe the table.

As she rinsed the cloth, she sincerely hoped there was never an occasion when she would be shrivelled by that same fierce expression aimed at her by Carrick Fitzhugh.

Lisa was by no account a coward, but she felt

certain she'd crumble to charred ashes if ever scorched by one of those looks from him.

Still, she vowed to herself, she would never be cowed, not by any living man, short or tall, breathtakingly attractive or average. So, naturally, when she turned around and found him watching her, she raised one eyebrow, angled her chin and gave him her most haughty expression…as if to say, *don't even try it, mister.*

For a moment, he look startled. Then the harshly set lines in his face smoothed. One corner of his mouth kicked up, as though he was fighting a grin.

Lisa narrowed her eyes, determined to continue meeting his steady stare.

A light, a glitter really, sparked to life in his eyes, a combined glint of challenge and a gleam of pure male sexual interest and intent.

It was one of the most difficult things Lisa had ever done, but somehow she managed to continue to hold his gaze, returning the silent challenge, while controlling nearly overwhelming, conflicting impulses either to dive for cover or into the shimmering depths of his deep-blue eyes.

Chapter 2

Magnificent.

The descriptive word swirled through Fitz's mind, in rhythm with the heat rushing through his body, converging on one particular part of him that surged in response.

Fitz shifted on the leather seat of his workhorse, a heavy-duty, four-wheel-drive, tan-and-dark-green truck, now crunching through the accumulating layer of still-falling snow.

Tan and green were his signature colors. They were on everything having to do with his business, from his stationery and letterhead to his pens and pencils, right down to the freebies he gave out year round, but especially during the local builders' association open-house week. Even his personal vehicle was dark green with tan interior.

Magnificent and beautiful and smart. Not the car, the woman. An Amazon, and a sexy-as-hell Amazon, at that.

Damn. He had big-time, hard-as-steel hots for Lisa Wolfe, had had them ever since he'd looked up from the blueprints of the Macdonoughs' house. Then it had been a tingly charge; now it felt like a raging electrical storm.

What a jolt. Fitz shook his head, a sense of wonder filling his mind. He hadn't felt this intensity of physical attraction for a woman in…

Hell, he couldn't recall ever before in his thirty-four years feeling this strongly aroused physically, emotionally or intellectually by any woman, not even the one he had rushed headlong to marry back in his early twenties, when he still believed in love…and fidelity.

Love. Fitz made a rude snorting noise. As the song title went, "What's Love Got to Do with It?" Love had gotten him nothing but emotional pain and the shock of rejection.

Who the hell needed that?

Not Fitz. He had been there, done that and paid the price of admission—and an even higher price to escape.

The sweet, petite, soft-voiced woman who had seemed hell-bent on setting a shopping record with

Fitz's money—damn hard-earned, at that—had turned into a complaining pain in the ass. She'd whined constantly about being left alone and ignored, with her shopping funds severely limited, while he busted *his* butt working to get his newly started business up and running and making a profit.

That was one of his former wife's irritating drawbacks, the one he hadn't learned about until after he was legally tied to her. She couldn't quite grasp the concept of needing actually to work and earn the money before you could spend it.

When she'd stopped responding to Fitz in bed, he had assumed, foolishly as it turned out, that she was withholding sex from him as a form of punishment. But it didn't take long for Fitz to realize that the real reason she was holding out on him was simply that she was giving out to another man.

Damn thing was, by then, Fitz no longer cared. In fact, he decided the poor jerk had done him a favor.

Nevertheless, it did cost him a bundle to get free of her. For, as Fitz found out, although the other guy, in his V.P. position for an major insurance firm, pulled down a plentiful salary—which "the witch" was happily squandering in all the best upscale shops—Fitz was left holding the bag, and the dubious honor of paying for the divorce.

Oh, for sure, he could have filed for the divorce, charged her with adultery, drawn the highly-paid jerk into the picture, let him pay the costs. He was sleeping with her, having sex with her, getting the connubial perks that were rightfully and legally due Fitz. So, he could have hired a P.I. to do his thing, get proof of their extra-curricular activities and stick the jerk with the costs.

Like hell.

What man worth the name wants the world to know he's being cuckolded, in his own bed, no less, after little more than a year and a half of marriage?

Fitz paid the bill.

Love, wasn't it grand?

In Fitz's admittedly rather bitter opinion, it wasn't worth spit, or even thinking about.

But lust…now, that was worth serious consideration. And he was considering it, very seriously. Shared lust with the blond, beautiful, slender, sexy Amazon with the fry-a-man's-mind and knot-up-his-shorts smile.

Yeaaah.

But indulging his lustful fantasies with the Amazon would not be a snap, easily accomplished. In just the few hours he had been in her company, Fitz had concluded that Lisa was very intelligent, savvy and wary. A formidable and challenging combination.

Fitz smiled as he pulled the growling monster truck into the driveway of his home, manhandled it around on the macadamed area in front of the three-car garage, and backed smoothly into one of the spacious bays.

He loved a challenge, any challenge, but most especially one posed by a gorgeous, independent, skeptical woman. And Lisa fit the description perfectly.

In fact, as he had decided around fifteen minutes after meeting her, she was simply magnificent.

Another thought jumped into his mind, and Fitz laughed aloud as he pressed the remote to lower the automatic garage doors. He ducked under them as they were closing and headed for the smaller building, an exact duplicate of his house, directly across the wide paved driveway. *Come to think of it, Mac's chili had come damn close to magnificent, too, but though good, excellent even, it paled in comparison to the statuesque blonde.*

"Every day?"

Lunch long since over and the kitchen restored to its usual neatness, Lisa and Matt were once again seated at the table, the blueprints spread out on the smooth surface.

"Yes." Matt was doing her best to educate Lisa on how to read and understand the layout of the plans.

Mac had left to visit a hospitalized parishioner soon after lunch, at the same time as Fitz had made his departure…after heaping praise on Mac for his culinary ability.

Matt rolled her eyes at Lisa's persistence. "Yes," she repeated. "Oh, of course, I don't expect you to go if this snow really piles up, but otherwise…" She shrugged. "You know it's fairly close by, and I certainly don't expect you to spend hours and hours there."

"Don't you trust Mr. Fitzhugh?" Lisa asked, frowning.

"Of course I do," Matt exclaimed. "Fitz has an excellent reputation in the trade. He was named builder of the year by the local home builders' association at their annual dinner just last week."

Glad to hear the man was well respected, even though she didn't want to delve into why she was glad, but more than a little baffled, Lisa shook her head. "Then, what am I missing here?"

"Missing?" Matt repeated.

"I don't get it," Lisa explained. "If you trust Fitz, why the daily visits? Especially by me. I don't know the first thing about building a house."

"Well…neither do I," Matt admitted. "But…"

"Then why go?" Lisa interrupted in exasperation. "If you trust Fitz, and don't know what you're looking at, or for, why bother with the daily round trips in the first place?" Lisa persisted, ever logical.

"It's not Fitz," Matt said, defensively. "But several friends have told me that it's advantageous to check on the progress of the work every day.''

''But why?'' Lisa demanded.

''Because, they said, you can't always trust some of the sub-contractors. A few have been known to fudge it, you know, like skimp on materials, or use cheaper, inferior-quality stuff to make a larger profit. And the buyer winds up with problems he didn't bargain for.''

''That's outrageous.'' The lawyer in Lisa rushed to the fore, ready to do battle for the innocent, unwary home buyer. Living in a high-rise condo, she hadn't a clue what went into building a home. ''And you trust Fitzhugh? How could you? How could anyone?'' Saying the words caused a pang in her chest. She didn't want to examine the possible reason for that twist of pain.

''Well...why shouldn't I?'' Matt said in exasperation. ''He's not the one fudging.''

''But he's the builder,'' Lisa argued. ''Doesn't he stay on top of his projects?''

''Yes, but not on a daily basis.'' Matt heaved a sigh. ''Jerry Clouser, Fitz's field supervisor, does a daily round of the sites.''

''Wouldn't he spot the 'fudging,' as you call it, if one of the sub-contractors was cheating?''

Matt shrugged. ''It depends.''

''On what?'' Lisa persisted, sounding not unlike

a terrier with a bone…or a lawyer in full verbal stride.

Matt heaved another, deeper sigh. "On how many houses they have under construction, and how much time Jerry can spend in each one every day."

"Well, that makes sense," Lisa conceded. "What doesn't make sense to me is, if his reputation is so sterling, why would Fitzhugh hire a questionable sub-contractor?"

"Lisa, really." Matt's tone was a combination of pleading and impatience. "Fitz wouldn't hire anyone whose honesty or quality of work was questionable," she paused to take a breath, rushing on before Lisa could get a word out, "But he would have to know first, wouldn't he?"

"I suppose." Lisa was again forced to concede the point as valid. "And, it does stand to reason that, as in any other business, even the law, there are those with very good work ethics who, through whatever mismanagement or folly, finding themselves in financial difficulties might give in to the temptation to fudge."

Matt let out a breath with a whoosh. "At last, the prosecution rests."

Lisa grinned. "Was I in my lawyer mode?"

"You just don't quit." Matt grinned back. "Do you?"

"No." Lisa shook her head. "You don't win

many cases by quitting." She grinned back at Matt. "Or anything else, come to think of it."

"True." Matt suddenly giggled. "Just think, if David and I had quit, we wouldn't be having twins, and it wouldn't have been nearly as much fun, either."

Lisa giggled with her, enjoying the familiar, but too rare sheer fun of being giggly with her sister again. "So, the two of you had fun, did you?"

"Bliss," Matt murmured, sobering. "It was wonderful. I can hardly wait until..." Her voice trailed away on a sigh of longing.

Lisa frowned, completely ignorant of the physical restrictions of pregnancy. "You and David can't...?" she began, only to be interrupted by her pouting sister.

"No, we can't have sex, just to be on the safe side," Matt said. "My doctor told us on our visit last week. She said it's too close to my time, and I'm too big."

"She's right there," Lisa said, trying to ignore another pang inside by studying Matt's very large belly. Surely she wasn't feeling envy for her sister...for the blissful intimacy she had shared with David, or the pregnancy that had resulted from it?

Was she suddenly beginning to hear her biological clock running? She, Lisa Wolfe, who had set aside all thoughts of marriage and children for the practice of law and her career?

Ridiculous. With that one word, Lisa rejected the idea of a ticking clock—and the strange pang.

Must be indigestion from David's delicious, but hot and spicy chili.

"So, are you going to stop staring at my belly and run over to the site?"

Matt's voice jolted Lisa from her unusual reverie. "You want me to go today, in the snow?"

"Oh, that's right." Matt frowned. "I completely forgot that it was snowing. I wonder if it's amounting to anything." She moved to heave herself from the chair, just as the kitchen door opened and David strolled into the room.

"It's stopped snowing, and there's about two inches on the ground. The roads are passable." He raised a chiding eyebrow at his wife. "You mustn't have missed me very much. You apparently weren't too concerned about the weather or about me out there in it."

Finally upright, Matt waddled to him, her eyes aglow with love and laughter. "You're right, I wasn't concerned about the weather." She curled her arms around his neck, cuddling as close as she could get to him. "But I'm always aware and concerned about you. Awake or asleep, safe inside or," the laughter sang in her voice, "outside in that cold, wet, nasty old weather."

David was laughing with his teasing wife.

Lisa was laughing, too...refusing to acknowledge the now familiar growing pang in region of her heart.

"If you two are going to get mushy, I'm getting out of here," Lisa said, heaving an exaggerated sigh. "I'll give you some privacy, David, if you'll give me the keys to the four-wheel. I'll drive out to the site to inspect the house...not that I have a clue what I'll be looking for."

Still holding on to his wife and still laughing, David tossed her the keys.

"You've only been to the site once," Matt said, stopping Lisa in her tracks as she started for the living room and the coat closet. "Do you remember the way?"

Lisa turned to give her sister a withering look. "Of course I remember the way. Didn't I spend time here every summer?" She didn't wait for an answer, but demanded, "Exactly where and when did you decide I was an idiot?"

Matt grinned, unimpressed with Lisa's withering look and tone. "Where? At the shallow creek that runs through the Simmons' pasture," she answered sweetly. "And when? The day you decided to go skinny-dipping in the creek, slipped on one stone and gashed your butt on another stone."

David roared with laughter.

"I was eleven," Lisa protested, fighting the urge to join David in laughter. "Besides, you were with me,'' she defended herself. ''And just as buck-naked as I was.''

''Ahhh, buck-naked, were you?'' David murmured, a wicked light in his eyes. ''And how many boys were there skinny-dipping as well?''

''David!'' Matt scolded, giggling.

''I'm outta here.'' Shaking her head in mock despair at the two of them, Lisa strode from the room.

Fitz had a hunch—or maybe just a hope.

From the latest reports, the weather was no longer a big deal. It had stopped snowing, leaving only a couple of inches on the ground. Instead of concentrating on his work, Fitz had been staring out his window, wondering if Lisa Wolfe had gone to the building site. He had noticed the traffic moving easily on the road in front of the office.

Hell, he might as well go have a look-see, he decided, shoving his desk chair back; he wasn't getting any work done staring out the window.

Striding from his spacious office on the second floor of the building, Fitz went along the short hall, down the steps, and into the reception area and showroom. He paused only long enough to stick his head through the doorway into his assistant/accounts officer/receptionist's office.

''Sherry, I'm going out to the Macdonough site,'' he said, drawing her attention from her computer.

"I shouldn't be gone long, page me if something comes up."

If something comes up.

Fitz laughed inside at his common, but also sexually suggestive phrase. As soon as he closed the office door behind him, his laughter escaped, the soft sound mingling with his breath cloud in the cold air.

Hell, if his hunch was right and Lisa was at the site, he didn't know how he could control "something coming up," or at the very least, something being stirred up.

"Friend, I think you have a bit of a problem," Fitz told himself, turning out of the driveway onto the already nearly cleared road. What the devil would he say to her? "Oh, hi, there, I didn't know you were coming today."

Oh, damn, Fitz swore to himself, shifting on the leather seat. There he went again with the unintentional but definitely double-entendre phrasing.

What the hell was it about this particular woman, anyway? he wondered, both confused and bemused by his so-sudden, so-intense response to her.

He had never felt anything near this depth of— whatever it was—for any other woman.

Which brought him full circle, Fitz thought, his pulse quickening as he neared the site. What was it about Lisa that had hit him like a fist to the midsection?

Sure she was beautiful. An inadequate description

if he had ever thought one. But, hell, he had known other beautiful women—Lisa's sister for one, since they were identical twins. He had known Matt for several years, soon after she and Mac had married, and, though he had admired her beauty, he had never felt in the least drawn to her in a personal or physical way.

It was wacko. How could one sister have no effect on him stronger than admiration and friendliness, while her identical twin turned him on so quickly at first sight?

Oh, sure, Lisa's cool, collected, I've-got-everything-under-control persona had a lot to do with his immediate attraction to her; Fitz did so love a challenge.

And she certainly did present a challenge. He had figuratively, if not literally, heard the gauntlet hit the table the moment his eyes met hers. The challenge was unspoken, but understood in the directness of her stare, the tilt of her chin.

Mac's vehicle was parked at the site.

A soft sigh of relief, a shiver of anticipation and a hope that Lisa had driven the SUV and not Matt or Mac, accompanied Fitz as he stepped from the truck and headed for the house.

Chapter 3

Lisa was inside the large walk-in closet in the master bedroom when she suddenly went still, a now familiar and growing chill, thrill, tremor...whatever, doing its thing up her spine at the sound of one of the voices rising up to her from the first floor.

"Hey, what are you doing here? Clouser sick or is something wrong?" That voice belonged to Bill Swartz, the painter who was laying a coat of white on the dining-room walls. When she'd arrived, not twenty minutes ago, he had understandably mistaken her for her sister until he noted her not-so-pregnant belly.

"No, Clouser's not sick, and nothing's wrong." That voice belonged to Carrick Fitzhugh, the only man whose voice had ever caused such weird feelings inside her.

"Is Ms. Wolfe here?"

Oh, yes, definitely Fitzhugh.

"Yeah, she's upstairs." Mr. Swartz laughed. "You know, she looks exactly like Mrs. Macdonough."

"Yeah, I know." Lisa trembled again at the sound of his first footstep on the stairs. "They're twins."

"As if anyone could miss it," Bill muttered.

Fitz laughed.

Lisa shivered, and seriously considered hiding there in the closet, just waiting, hoping he'd go into one of the other rooms, so she could then run down the stairs and out the door.

Run? The very idea shot steel into her spine. Damned if she would run from any man, even if he did give her the hot-and-cold running shivers.

The footsteps stopped; she held her breath.

"There's a thin spot, over there in the southwest corner, Bill," Fitz pointed out.

Lisa resumed breathing.

"Damned if you ain't right," Bill muttered. "You don't miss anything, do you?"

"Not much," Fitz agreed, without a trace of boasting in his tone. "Good thing, too. Keeps all of us working."

"You're right about that, too." Bill laughed.

His footsteps started again.

The hot-and-cold running chills started again, too.
He stopped on the landing. "Lisa?"

She slid one foot back, then recalling Bill, within
hailing distance in the dining room, she straightened
her shoulders, raised her chin, and walked out of the
closet. "I'm in the master bedroom," she called.

"So you are," he drawled.

The sight of him stopped her cold one step inside
the room.

He stood in a casual-looking stance, his long body
propped against the door frame. A shadow of a smile
played over his lips, drawing her gaze from his body
to his mouth. His mouth. Lisa smothered a groan of
protest against the sizzle of awareness crackling between them.

The giant was simply too damned attractive, too
damned masculine and much too damned sexy. The
thrill and tingle drained from her spine to coil around
her hips, sparking an aching heat in the core of her
femininity.

"You feel it, too. Don't you?" His voice was low,
pure seduction.

Determined not to melt onto the carpet...or into
his strong, muscular arms, Lisa gathered her consid-
erable inner strength and poise around her like a
cloak. "The chill in here from the lack of heat?"
She even managed a smile of sheer bravado. "Yes,
of course I feel it."

He laughed.

Oh, gee, she wished he wouldn't do that; the sound of his deep, sensuous laughter was nearly her undoing.

Silently cursing him, Lisa soldiered on. "When does the heater get installed?"

"It is installed, and working," he said, motioning to the vent along the baseboard. "The vents are closed in here, because this room's finished. It's warm downstairs." He arched an eyebrow. "Didn't you feel it when you came in?"

In truth, Lisa *had* noticed, but torture short of pulling out her teeth or nails wouldn't make her admit it to him. "I guess I was still cold from outside," she sidestepped.

"Humm." He nodded, then threw her a curve. "You want to go out to dinner this evening?"

"With you?" Caught off-guard, Lisa blurted it out without thinking.

"No, with Bill downstairs. Of course, his wife might object." He grinned. "Yes, with me."

"I...ah..." Why wouldn't the resounding "no" she wanted to say come out of her mouth? Was she hesitating because he and David and Matt were friends?

Amusement lit his eyes. "Is that a yes or a no?"

Friends or not, in self-defense, she was going to reject his offer.

"Yes, I'll go to dinner with you," Lisa answered, actually managing to stun herself.

She must be losing her tiny little mind, Lisa decided. That was the only excuse for her response. Wary, she watched as his grin grew into a real, breath-stealing smile.

"Good," he said, his broad chest moving in slow exhalation, almost as if in relief.

Yeah, right, Lisa chided herself. This gorgeous man probably had women falling all over him. Somehow she couldn't picture him being relieved that one woman agreed to have a simple meal with him.

"What time?"

His question jarred her from her thoughts. What time? Oh, he meant for dinner. No longer any doubt, she thought, feeling impatient with herself and her unusual lack of mental agility. She *was* losing her tiny little mind.

"That's unimportant to me," she said, assuring herself and conveying to him that, indeed, neither the time nor the actual date itself were important. "What time is good for you?"

Fitz was no longer smiling, and the glint of challenge was back in his eyes. "I'm usually in my office until six. Would seven be okay?"

"Yes, fine." Suddenly realizing she was still standing nearly in the closet doorway, she forced herself to turn and move toward him. "I must go now." She walked to within a foot of him.

Fitz didn't move, but continued to stand there, lazily propped against the door frame, watching her every step like a hungry predator.

"Why?" His voice was soft, enticing. "You haven't seen the entire house. Have you?"

Lisa came to a full stop. A wash of awareness swept over her. Damned if she couldn't smell him, the musky scent of his perspiration, the sexual male power of him. Keeping her cool was just one more challenge.

Determined to meet it, at all costs, Lisa lifted her chin, offered him a patently false smile and lied through her teeth. "Yes, I have." She was rather proud of the haughty tone she had manufactured. "Now, if you'll excuse me?"

"Ahhh, sweetheart," he said in a seductive murmur. "I'd probably excuse you just about anything."

Telling herself she would not be affected by a half promise he didn't mean, Lisa stepped to him, tapped a slender index finger against his rock-hard chest and tipped her head up to look him straight in the eye.

"That's nice," she murmured back, her tone dry as day-old toast. "I'll keep it in mind. But right now, if you'll move it, I must leave."

He laughed. Damn him. Moving with deliberate, taunting slowness he straightened and backed away.

Lisa held on to a sigh of relief and swept past him with the regal bearing of a queen...at least she hoped her bearing was regal. Maybe not, considering she went down the stairs and out the front door as if devil dogs were snapping at her heels. His laughing voice called after her, making her pause as she was closing the door.

"Don't forget. Seven o'clock."

As if she could forget, no matter how much she wanted to, not just dinner, but ever having met him. He unnerved her, and Lisa didn't appreciate being unnerved. It messed up her self-image of clear-thinking control.

Lord save him, he did enjoy sparring with that woman, Fitz thought, staring after her. He was still laughing to himself as he strolled down the stairs.

"The painting okay upstairs, Fitz?" Bill asked anxiously, sticking his head around the dining-room archway.

"Looked okay to me," Fitz said, hoping it was, as he hadn't even glanced at the paint.

Bill exhaled and smiled. "Good."

Feeling great, Fitz smiled back. "I'm on my way. Have to get back to the office. See you later, Bill." With a casual wave, he crossed the kitchen and exited through the side door to the garage.

All the way back to the office, Fitz ruminated on where to take Lisa for dinner. It sure wasn't going to be the diner out on the highway, where he often stopped to eat on his way home from the office.

Not that there was anything wrong with the diner. It was clean and the food was good. And maybe sometime he'd take her there for a meal, maybe lunch, but not for dinner, and especially not tonight.

Tonight had to be someplace special, a place with more than excellent cuisine, a place with ambience and atmosphere, muted lighting, soft music and candles on the table.

Inspiration struck. The Mansion Inn, some seven or eight miles outside Sprucewood. It was an actual mansion that had sat empty for years, slowly deteriorating. Fitz had known about the place ever since it had been bought and restored to its former glory some ten or so years before. He knew the food was superb, having been there for the first time to attend a friend's birthday dinner two weeks before Christmas.

Yep, the Mansion Inn fit the bill for his first date with Lisa. It was the perfect setting for what he hoped would be a romantic dinner for two. And the best part of it was, Fitz had never taken another woman there.

Too bad Lisa would be returning to Denver sometime after David and Matt's twins were born, because Fitz would surely love to see her during the summer and maybe even go skinny-dipping with her.

He was so distracted by the thought of the oh-so-cool Lisa Wolfe, reputedly fierce attorney at law, bare-butt naked, breathtaking in nothing but her own satin-soft skin, Fitz had to laugh at himself when he almost drove right by his own home and office building.

"You're losing it, Fitzhugh," he muttered aloud, stepping from the truck and striding across the parking area of the driveway. "If you don't watch it, you're liable to find yourself falling for the woman. Then what'll you do?"

Falling? Like, in love?

Naw. Fitz shook his head in denial as he mounted the stairs to his private office.

He had never been in love. Not really emotionally and physically in love. Hell, he wasn't sure he believed in love at all. But, if that were the case, what about couples like his own parents and David and Matt? If they weren't in love, deeply in love with each other...

Fitz shook his head again to clear his mind of speculation. What did it matter, anyway? He had no intention of falling in love, not with Lisa or any other woman. In two, three months at most, Lisa would be leaving to go back to Colorado, to her home and her work and her friends. Maybe men friends.

Fitz didn't particularly like the twist inside that that latest, unsettling thought gave him.

"Hi, I'm back," Lisa called as she walked into her sister's warm, aromatic kitchen. She didn't know what was baking in the oven, but it certainly did smell good. Maybe she could call Fitz up and cancel their dinner date, since her acceptance had been, if not strictly then certainly *almost* coerced. She didn't really want to go with him.

Did she?

The question gave her pause for thought. She really hadn't had to agree to go with him, and in all honesty, Fitz hadn't coerced her in the least. He had simply stood there, looking too attractive for her own good, in a quilted vest over a flannel work shirt tucked into the low-slung waistband of skin-tight jeans.

She shivered, darned if she still didn't have the musky scent of him teasing her senses.

"Hi, Lisa," Matt called, her voice sounding kind of fuzzy. "I'm in the living room."

Concerned by the note of blurriness in her sister's voice, Lisa hurried from the room, dropping her purse onto the dining table as she passed.

Alarm flared on sight of Matt struggling to push herself upright on the sofa from a prone position. Her apprehension must have been plain on her face. "Matt?" she exclaimed, rushing to her.

"Now...don't...panic," Matt said between quick breaths. "I'm fine." She stopped struggling, half lying, half sitting, and heaved a sigh. "Help me to sit up, please."

"Grab hold," Lisa said, grasping Matt's hands. Slowly, gently, she tugged Matt upright. "Better?"

"Yes." Matt's breathing began to ease. "So, how was everything at the house?"

"Fine, I guess." Lisa shrugged. "Not that I'd know if everything wasn't fine. There was a Bill Swartz there, painting the dining-room walls."

"Oh, good. Sounds like they're making progress." She was still slightly out of breath from her efforts.

Lisa frowned. "Honey, are you sure you're okay? No pains or backache?"

"Yes, I'm sure." Matt's breathing was now close to normal, and her sense of humor was intact. "I am not in labor." She grinned. "But it was worth the struggle just to see you rattled, it happens so rarely. I just have trouble getting up once I'm lying down on the sofa."

"Then why do you lie on the sofa?"

Matt made a face. "Because David insists I rest in the afternoon, and I hate crawling into bed in the daytime." Her grin took on a devilish slant. "That is, unless I'm crawling into bed to make love with David."

"Which your doctor has forbidden until after the babies are safely here," Lisa said, trying not to think of two people writhing on a mussed bed...especially as the two people in mind were not Matt and David, but herself and...stop it, she commanded her errant imagination.

"Yeah, bummer," Matt groused, in a good-natured way. "Who knew she was such a spoil-sport?"

Lisa laughed at her sister's gripe and her expression. She held out her hands. "Come on, petulant one, I'll help you to stand up. We'll go to the kitchen and I'll fix a pot of decaf coffee for us."

"Oh, goody," Matt said in aggrieved tones. "A treat of decaf coffee."

"Come on, Matt," Lisa chided, laughing at her sister's act of self-pity. Matt had never in her life suffered the pangs of self-pity. Come to that, neither had Lisa. "The decaf coffee you've been serving is really very good."

"That's the holiday spice coffee." Matt had dropped the playacting and returned to her normal cheeriness. "I love it. I hope I can get more, now that the holidays are over."

"Talking about the holidays," Lisa said from the counter where she was pouring water into the cof-feemaker, "got anymore of Gram's cookies?"

"Ohhh," Matt sighed dramatically. "I was hoping you wouldn't ask. I was saving them for a soli-tary binge."

Lisa gave her a dry look. "Too bad, kiddo, break them out, it's been a while since lunch." She hesi-tated, drew a calming breath, and said in as light a tone as she could muster, "Speaking about food. What's in the oven that smells so good?"

Matt was stretched out, her arm reaching into a

cabinet for the stashed cookies. "Pot roast," she said, her voice muffled by the cabinet door.

"Ahh…umm, I won't be here," Lisa said, as casually as if she had missed meals regularly since she'd been staying with them. Except for when they all had been visiting relatives during the holidays, she hadn't missed any.

"Won't be here?" Matt backed away from the cabinet, the precious cookies in her hand. She frowned. "Why not? Where are you going?"

"Carrick Fitzhugh invited me to have dinner with him," she answered in a rush.

Matt's face lit up. "Oh, that's wonderful."

No, it's scary, Lisa thought.

"Fitz is a nice guy," Matt went on enthusiastically. "I'm sure you'll enjoy yourself."

Lisa was equally sure she wouldn't, but she wasn't about to tell her sister that and wipe the brightness from her face. "Yes, I'm sure I will," she lied, wondering if lying to one's identical twin could really be considered a sin.

"When did you talk to Fitz, Lis?" Matt looked puzzled. "I didn't hear anything about dinner while he was here."

"I know." Lisa carefully poured out the coffee, loathing the slight tremor in her hands. Fortunately, Matt was too busy placing cookies on a plate to notice. "He showed up at the house while I was there."

"See." Matt's expression was smug. "I told you he checks the progress and the workmanship of his houses."

"Yes," Lisa conceded with a silent sigh. "You did. He's got a keen eye," she granted, without hesitation. "With a mere glance, he spotted a thin spot in the paint in one corner of the dining-room wall."

"That's our Fitz," Matt said, settling into a chair.

That's *your* Fitz, Lisa thought, carrying the steaming cups to the table. Leave me out of it.

A few minutes before seven, Lisa was still fussing with the intricate figure eight she had twisted her hair into; it was as close to perfect as one could hope for, yet she was still fussing with it...killing time, actually. She had dressed with care, but then, she always dressed with care. Not having a hint of where Fitz might be taking her, Lisa had dressed to fit almost any occasion. She had put on a white lace overblouse and a black full-length skirt. Two-inch-high black pumps, a black beaded evening bag and a twisted strand of black-and-white pearls with matching earrings finished off her ensemble.

She felt nervous, which wasn't like her at all, and a little scared, which definitely wasn't like her. The problem was that Lisa didn't know if she was scared of Fitzhugh or herself. A sorry state to be in.

She grew stiff when the doorbell rang. Her heart gave a tiny fluttering sensation at the sound of his voice. She didn't want to go with him! Instead, she wanted to have a light snack, a hot shower and crawl into bed with a good book...alone.

Pride forbade her from keeping him waiting. Squaring her shoulders, she left the room, moved along the short hallway and started down the stairs.

Fitz was standing right inside the door talking to Matt and David. At the soft sound of her footsteps on the stairs, he glanced up...and appeared to freeze in place.

A spark set a fire in the depths of his eyes, thawing him enough to move. Without taking his compelling gaze from her eyes, he walked to the foot of the staircase, held up his hand for hers to help her down the last two steps. His hand was warm, sending hot tingles up her arm.

"You look beautiful."

His low-pitched voice had the power of an explosion, sending shards of fiery emotional shrapnel throughout her body.

"Thank you." Lisa would never know how that smooth tone came out of her rough throat. "You look very nice yourself," she returned the compliment. She withdrew the hand he was still holding; his touch heating up her palm and her arm...and other, more intimate parts of her anatomy.

Nice was the height of understatement. Attired in a dark-gray suit, pale-blue shirt and red-and-silver striped tie, he looked good enough to...

Don't go there, Lisa warned herself, moving away to slip into the coat David was holding for her. Moving even faster, Fitz lifted the ankle-length black garment from David and gently draped it over her shoulders, his fingertips just lightly brushing over the back of her neck, gently ruffling the short hairs at her nape.

Somehow, Lisa found the fortitude to suppress the shiver his touch had created inside her, and the agility to step quickly away. The shiver she had fought so hard to contain now trembled throughout her body at the mocking sound of his soft laughter close to her ear.

Geez, Lisa asked herself, was that what she was in for for the rest of the evening—barely-there caresses and soft laughter? She moved smartly to the door at the light touch of his guiding hand at her waist. Even through her cashmere coat, she could feel the warmth of his hand. He was too close—the crisp, heady scent of his cologne scrambled her brain.

Well, that settled it. On the spot, Lisa decided that the question which had plagued her since practically their first meeting was no longer in doubt: she *was* out of her tiny little mind, or at the very least, damn close to it!

Fortunately, considering Lisa's choice of footwear, David had thoroughly cleared the walkway and the driveway. There wasn't a speck of snow left on either. Grateful to her brother-in-law for saving her from having to walk on tiptoe, and to the bitter cold for giving her a creditable reason for haste, she strode away from Fitz's stirring nearness, to the car at the end of the walk.

While almost certain that Fitz wouldn't have invited her to dine with him, then pick her up in his work truck, Lisa had vaguely imagined he would drive an SUV for his personal use. That wouldn't have bothered her in the least, since she herself drove one of the scaled-down models. She was pleasantly surprised, therefore, when he moved around her to open the passenger-side door of an American-made, mid-sized car. That the vehicle was a luxury model, dark green with a tan interior and equipped with all the bells and whistles, came as no surprise at all.

Fitz had left the motor running. The car was warm, as was the seat she slid into. Lovely. Clicking her seat belt, Lisa settled into the butter-soft leather comfortably...for all of the few seconds required for Fitz to circle the car and slide behind the wheel next to her.

In the small warm area, the tangy masculine scent of him drenched her senses. Suddenly the roomy car was too confined, too warm. Lisa felt as if the heated seat was scorching her posterior.

"Comfortable?"

Lisa nearly betrayed herself by starting at the quiet sound of his voice.

"Very. Thank you," she said. About as comfortable as sitting on hot stones, she thought.

"Good." He shot a quick smile at her. "It won't take us long to get there."

"Where is 'there'?" She flashed a quick smile back at him. Positive that her action had gone unnoticed by him, she was puzzled by the sudden tightening of his grip on the wheel.

"It's a place called the Mansion Inn, some six or so miles down the highway," Fitz answered, giving his full attention to the roadway.

"Mansion Inn," Lisa repeated, watching in fascination the play of light from the oncoming cars on his chiseled features. "It sounds impressive."

"Yeah." Fitz nodded. "I've been there only once, but the food was excellent."

Finding herself wondering who the woman was he had squired that evening, and not appreciating the odd little twinge she felt in her stomach, Lisa distracted herself by trying to imagine the decor of the restaurant.

With a name like *Mansion Inn,* she figured it was very likely elegant, opulent and probably Victorian.

She figured wrong.

Chapter 4

The Mansion Inn was a true mansion by any standards. Early American in design, it was not unlike Mount Vernon, only larger and without the outbuildings.

There was a valet attendant ready to take the car and park it. Three broad steps led up to the front door. Another employee was waiting to give them entrance.

"Impressive," Lisa murmured as they mounted the steps.

"Makes you feel important," Fitz agreed, flashing a teasing grin at her. "Even if you're not."

The door opened, Lisa took two steps inside, and stopped dead in her tracks, her startled gaze sweeping the large entrance area. She moved forward automatically at a gentle nudge from Fitz.

She caught a glimpse of the dining room to their left. As in the hallway, the decor was eighteenth-century, upper-class American, yet homey and inviting, not at all pretentious or overstated.

"This isn't at all what I'd imagined." Her quiet tones held a note of delighted surprise.

"What had you imagined?" Fitz asked, sliding the coat from her shoulders. "Something fancy?"

"Yes," she admitted, slipping her arms from the coat sleeves. "Elegant and posh. Victorian, actually."

He laughed, and handed the garment to the young woman behind the coat-check counter. From there, he cupped Lisa's elbow to lead her to the host's station positioned at a wide entranceway into the spacious dining room.

"Well, it's your fault. When you told me..." she began in self-defense, only to be interrupted by the host.

"Good evening, sir, madam." The maître d' was in his late fifties or early sixties. He was tall, slender, and quite handsome for a man his age. "You have reservations?" One silvery eyebrow rose up his forehead, toward a full head of silvery hair. His voice was silvery as well. His suit was dark, his shirt crisp white, his tie every bit as silvery as his hair... naturally.

"Yes." Fitz's voice was clipped, edgy. "Under Fitzhugh, party of two."

Startled out of her admiration for the man's impeccable appearance, Lisa gave Fitz a quick glance, confused by his sharp tone, his aggressive stance.

"Of course," the host said, smoothly. Picking up two huge menus, he turned away. "If you'll follow me."

Still bemused by Fitz's odd manner, Lisa trailed after the host. Fitz trailed close behind her...too close. She could feel his warmth from the fine, quivering hairs at her nape to the very base of her spine. And there it was again, that heady, tangy, masculine scent that tantalized her senses.

Why was it she had never before felt such a powerful impact from a man's warmth, nearness, his scent?

Distracted by her thoughts, Lisa gave a faint smile and a murmured "Thank you" to the host as he seated her and then handed her one of the menus.

"Robert will be your server this evening. He'll be with you momentarily." Without so much as a glance at Fitz, the host bowed and stepped back. "Enjoy your dinner."

Though Lisa murmured another thank-you, her attention was centered on Fitz's narrow-eyed, stone-faced expression as he watched the host walk away.

"What was that all about?" she asked, the minute the man was out of earshot.

"What was what all about?" Fitz turned back to look at her, all signs of the hardness in his eyes and in his face gone. His expression was now pleasant, innocent.

Innocent. Lisa almost laughed out loud. She strongly suspected Fitz had long ago outgrown innocence.

"You know what," Lisa chided him. "Your attitude and barely civil manner with the host."

Fitz blessed her, tormented her, with the most beguiling smile she had ever seen. A heating sensation flared to life inside her, too deep inside her. Her breath catching in her throat, Lisa thought about Colorado blizzards, mounds and mounds of snow. It helped a bit to cool the fire...but not much.

"Barely civil?" His smile dissolved into soft laughter that melted the mounds and mounds of snow she had piled up inside her head. "Then, you should be relieved to know that being barely civil was nothing compared to what I really wanted to do to the smarmy phony."

Lisa was almost afraid to ask, but she had to know. "What did you really want to do?"

"Knock the creep on his ass." Blunt and to the point: it fitted Fitz perfectly.

Lisa stared at him in puzzlement. "But...why?"

Fitz again went for blunt. "Why? Because, when

we first came in, and you were checking out the decor, Mr. Self-Important Twerp was checking out your figure.''

"You're kidding." Lisa was hard put to keep from laughing, but she lost the battle of the amused twitch at the corners of her lips. "I hope he appreciated the view."

"What?"

Stumped him. Lisa felt a surge of pleasure. She had actually stumped him. "The view," she enunciated. "I hope he appreciated it. I work my butt off in the gym three days a week, and run every morning, weather permitting, when I'm at home. Since I've been here, I've been doing my aerobics and running on Matt and David's treadmill in the basement."

Fitz laughed aloud; the sound was even more beguiling and exciting than his smile. "You're something, Lisa Wolfe, you know that?"

"Sure." She shrugged. Why bother with false modesty? She knew what she was, what she looked like. She didn't even need to look into a mirror. "How could I not know? All I need do is look at my sister. In addition, and also quite like Matt, I have a generous share of intelligence, and a pretty good sense of humor, to boot."

He was grinning at her bluntness.

"And you're something, as well, Carrick Fitzhugh," she returned the compliment—at any rate, she decided to treat it as a compliment. "You know that?"

"Sure." His grin flashed again, then it was gone. His gaze was intent, his expression serious. "It's just as I figured. We'll be terrific together."

Lisa refrained from asking. She knew precisely what he had meant by *we* and *together*. The image those two words created in her mind was at the same time scary, exciting and too explicit for her own good. Telling herself to pull her senses into order, Lisa raised her chin and met his intense look, stare for stare. "You're pretty sure of yourself." To her amazement, and relief, her voice was cool, detached. "Aren't you?"

"Oh, yeah," he agreed, his gaze delving into hers. "We'll be together in as many ways as there are for a man and woman to be together. Maybe not tonight, or even tomorrow night, but in the not-too-distant future. I want to be with you so badly the soles of my feet tingle. And I believe you want me every bit as much as I want you."

Good heavens! Feeling hot, flustered, chills using her spine for a playground slide, the soles of her feet beginning to tingle, Lisa glanced around at the neighboring tables, hoping to hell that none of the occupants had overheard him. She sighed in relief to note that not one person was staring in shock, smirking or even paying the slightest attention to them.

"Are you crazy?" she demanded, in a rough murmur. "What if someone had heard you?"

"What if?" He shrugged. "I'm not ashamed of the way I feel. Sexual attraction between a man and a woman is a natural thing." He gave her a slow, sexy smile. "Makes the world go round, not to mention keeping it populated."

"Really?" Lisa said, arching one blond brow, while sliding one foot out of her shoe to rub it against the carpet in hopes of brushing away the tingle. Instead, the friction only increased the sensation. "I'll concede that sexual attraction is natural, and increases the population. But I was also led to believe that love made the world go 'round." Her tones were dry, cynical, her gaze steady on his.

"Could happen," he concurred, just as dryly.

Wary, but curious, she asked, "What could happen?"

"You, me, terrific in bed together, and in love."

"I don't think so," Lisa said. Actually she nearly choked it out. "I don't believe in romantic love." Except for her parents, she thought. And Matt and David. And her uncles and aunts. And her grandmother and deceased grandfather. And her cousins who were married, or about to be.

Oh, hell.

Fitz had been watching her, the play of emotions on her face, like a hawk. Lisa fervently hoped she had not revealed her thoughts to him.

"I don't, either."

She blinked. "Don't what?"

"Believe in romantic love. But who knows?" His broad shoulders rippled again in a light shrug. "As I said, it could happen."

"Don't bet your business on it," she warned, uncertain if the warning was for him or herself.

He smiled.

She swallowed a groan against the inner melting sensation. Damn his smile, his eyes, the magnetic attraction of him. Lisa was raking her mind, with little success, for some effectively discouraging remark, when she was saved the effort by the overdue arrival of the server at their table.

"Good evening, I'm Robert, your server." He was young, tall and lean, with a pleasant face and bleached blond hair. "I'm truly sorry for the delay, but there was a bit of confusion in the kitchen. May I bring you something to drink?"

Relieved, her throat feeling tight and parched, Lisa flashed a brilliant smile at Robert in gratitude to him for ending the unsettling dialogue between her and Fitz.

"Yes," she answered with a soundless sigh. "I'll have a glass of white zinfandel with ice now, and a glass of iced water with my dinner, please."

Robert returned her smile, then shifted it to Fitz. "And you, sir?"

Fitz smiled back. "I'll have the same as the lady,"

his smile grew into a quick grin. "But forget the ice, not in the water, in the wine."

"Yes, sir," Robert said, laughing softly as he moved to fill their order.

"You like your wine watered down?"

Doubly relieved that he didn't revert to their previous conversation, Lisa rewarded him with her sweetest smile. "I don't dislike it that way," she said. "What I do like is keeping my mind clear and alert."

"Good. So do I." He gifted her with another of his stomach-clenching smiles. "I appreciate a woman who, like me, is wise enough to keep her senses together, and is fully aware of what she is doing at all times of the day...and night."

Lisa knew what he was saying between the lines, as precisely as if he had shouted aloud. He didn't want to make love with a woman sloshed out of her mind, who, afterward, made a fuss, claiming not to have known what she was doing.

She opened her mouth to respond...but nothing came out. On the surface, his statement had sounded innocuous enough. Fitz was watching her, waiting. What could she say?

Once again Robert saved her.

"Your wine," he said, setting the stemmed glasses in front of them. "Are you ready to order?"

Order? Oh, Lord. Lisa hadn't given the menu a

glance. "Ahh, no." She offered him a weak smile. "If we could have a few more minutes?"

"Of course." He began to turn away.

"Just a second," Fitz said, not an order, a request. "I know what I want, so while the lady's making her choice, I wonder if you'd explain something to me."

"Yes, sir, if I can," Robert said, glancing at the menu as if certain the question pertained to a particular dish.

Fitz's voice was low. "What was the 'bit of confusion in the kitchen' you mentioned?"

Robert glanced around him, an impish smile playing over his lips, a devilish glint in his eyes. "The chef," he said in a near whisper. "He was having a hissy fit, bringing everyone to a dead stop, because one of the newer cooks overcooked the white asparagus."

Fitz laughed, drawing smiles from their neighbors, a grin from Robert and a shiver through Lisa. "I like it overcooked. If the chef hasn't tossed it out with the cook, I'll have some, along with the broiled salmon steak. And I'll start with the mixed salad with the house dressing."

"Very good, sir." He shifted his glance to Lisa, but before he could speak Fitz cut in.

"Have you decided, Lisa, or would you like a few minutes more?"

"Yes, I've decided," she said from behind the

large menu, where she'd been hiding her smile at Robert's answer, and Fitz's response. "I'll start with the salad with an oil and balsamic vinegar dressing and I'll have the broiled scallops with the asparagus, if available."

"Yes, ma'am." Still grinning, he walked away.

A silence stretched taut and strained between them for a few moments. Fitz frowned and heaved a sigh. Lisa began to grow uneasy. "Is something wrong?"

"I am really annoyed." He looked it. His tone was one of quiet outrage. "Can you believe it?"

"Believe what?" Now she was frowning, not in annoyance but in complete confusion.

His eyes took on a teasing gleam. "That the cook overcooked the white asparagus," he ranted. "That's what."

Lisa lost it. Unfortunately, she had just taken a sip of the wine. Grabbing the napkin from her lap, she raised it to her mouth, afraid she would either spew wine all over the table, or choke. She wasn't sure which was worse. Yet, somehow, she managed to avoid both embarrassing reactions. Controlling her laughter, she swallowed the wine. Then she laughed.

He laughed with her, once again drawing smiles from the patrons surrounding them.

The taut silence between them dissolved with their combined laughter. Feeling the tension drain from her body, Lisa sighed and relaxed.

"That's better."

"Better?" Lisa gave him a puzzled look, even though she felt sure she knew what he meant. But, it had to be her turn to tease. "What's better? The fact that neither one of us minds overcooked asparagus?"

"Well, that, too." He smiled. "But I was referring to the fact that you finally appear to be enjoying yourself." He raised his brows. "Does that surprise you?"

Should she be candid, or dance around an answer? Lisa gave a mental shrug. Go for candid.

"I am enjoying myself." She smiled back at him with surprising ease. "Finally."

"I'm sorry if I made you uncomfortable before." He sounded sincerely contrite, but that warning gleam was back in his eyes. "And for rudely ordering my meal before you."

"Apology accepted," Lisa said, shaking her head in despair at herself for again being unable to contain the laughter bubbling up inside of her.

Who knew, who would ever have dreamt he'd be such fun to be with, banter with? And, amazingly, even with their unsettling if alluring conversation earlier, she was already looking forward to future meetings with him. Lisa was startled by the thrill of excitement and anticipation the thought sent skittering through her body.

"Ahhh…" Fitz murmured in appreciation, his

glance shifting over her shoulder. "Here come our dinners. At last, the overcooked white asparagus."

The meal was expertly prepared and delicious, Lisa thought later, dabbing at her lips with the cloth napkin. She was rather surprised at the sight of her empty plate. Even the dreaded and much-maligned white asparagus had been delicious.

She skipped dessert. Fitz didn't. Seemingly without a care, he slowly devoured his mouthwatering, calorie-laden chocolate mousse, relishing every spoonful. His eyes laughed at her every time he stuck the spoon in his mouth.

Lisa loved chocolate. It was one of her weaknesses, one she vigorously fought on a daily basis. Apparently, Fitz had figured that out, most likely from the envious expression on her face every time he lifted the spoon.

"Would you like a taste?" he asked, scooping up a spoonful and holding it out to her. "A tiny taste?"

"Sadist," she muttered in contrived tones of disapproval, glaring at him.

"Me?" He popped the spoon into his mouth. "Not I," he denied, drawing it out slowly, curling his tongue around the shallow bowl. "Next best thing to great sex," he assured her. "Chocolate, that is."

The thrill of excitement, like an electric shock, sizzled through her, from her tingling lips to the still-tingling soles of her feet.

Lisa had seen performances of sensuality similar to his before, on TV, in movies and even a few times in cafés and restaurants. She had always had the same reaction to the less-than subtle displays. Oh, brother, she had thought, was any woman ever truly affected by such an overt play? And, if so, did these women have a brain in their heads?

Did *she?* Apparently not, because, like it or not—and Lisa definitely did not like it—Fitz's innocent-looking move had the uncomfortable effect of a live wire zinging through every atom of her body.

No, she most assuredly didn't like the sensation, or the intense way he was watching her; a large bird of prey came to mind. Stormed by mixed emotions—excitement, embarrassment, dismay—she lowered her eyes to her after-dinner cup of rapidly cooling coffee.

She should be so lucky.

"Lisa?" His voice was soft, pure enticement. "Is anything wrong?"

"Not at all," Lisa said. Everything, she thought, raising her head to meet his intent gaze.

"Are you sure?" he persisted. "You look a lit-tle…" he shrugged "…I don't know, upset, angry."

Lisa found a reasonable facsimile of a smile. "No, Fitz, I am neither upset nor angry." She thought it prudent not to admit to feeling… What? A little breathless, fluttery, with a strange sensation of anticipation? No it wouldn't be at all prudent, not to mention smart, to say that.

"Would you like to go somewhere from here?" he asked, taking her at her word. "We could see a late movie, or there's a club—a low-key club and *nice*," he emphasized, "not too far from here, with a dance floor."

Oh, sure, Lisa thought, groaning inwardly. That was all she needed—to dance with him, his body against hers. She knew if she danced with him, it *would* be his body against hers, tightly against hers.

Oh, no. Dancing was out of the question. It was time to make a dignified retreat, gather her rattled wits together. The jumble of emotions and sensations she was experiencing were so uncharacteristic of her, she wasn't quite certain how to handle them, how to handle *him*. Yet. But she'd sort it out, as soon as she was alone.

"Thinking it over?" Fitz softly asked, nudging her from her reverie. "Or falling asleep?"

Lisa couldn't help smiling at him, the amusement underlying his quiet tone. Little did he know he had handed her a perfect excuse to decline.

"Yes and no," she said. "I was thinking it over, and I wasn't falling asleep, although I must confess I very easily could have done so."

He flashed his devastating grin. "Boring company?"

"No." Lisa shook her head, laughing. He was far

from boring. Just the opposite; he was far too interesting, exciting, never mind sexy. "It's been a long day," she explained. "I was up very early to drive my parents to the airport. Then, when I got back to Matt's after inspecting the house, for all the good that did me, or her, I nearly had a heart attack to find her lying on the sofa, struggling to get up, as if in distress."

He jerked erect in his chair. "She's all right, isn't she? I mean—" he went on before she could utter a word of assurance "—Matt seemed fine when we left, and David was calm."

"David's always calm," Lisa said, her smile soft. "And, yes, Matt's fine, too. Turns out David has insisted she have a rest in the afternoon, and though she was struggling to get upright on the sofa, it was because of her unbalanced size, not distress."

"Whew, that's a relief." Fitz sighed, then laughed. "And you're right about David. I've never seen him un-calm." He grinned again. "If there is such a word."

"I'm not sure, but I seriously doubt it." She shrugged. "Who knows? Anyway, after I recovered from the scare over Matt, I did my regular one-hour exercise routine. Now I think the length and events of the day have caught up with me." She naturally didn't add that the longest, and the shortest most eventful hours of all had been the few hours she had spent in his disturbing company.

"In other words, you'd like me to take you home."

"Yes, please."

Tension began to crawl through Lisa the minute Fitz closed the car door after seating her. Questions chased themselves around in her mind, coiling the tension tighter inside her with each passing mile. He was quiet, seemingly distracted, which didn't help break the mental circle of questions.

Would he try to kiss her when the got to Matt and David's house?

Would she let him?

Would he ask her out again?

Would she agree to go with him?

Would he try to kiss her?

Would she let him?

The tension wound so tightly inside her, Lisa was half afraid she'd fly apart in fifteen different directions.

Would he try to kiss her?

Lord, she hoped so.

No, she didn't. She wasn't sure she could stand it.

For pity's sake, stop it, Lisa chastised herself. She was as worked up as an innocent and shy, retiring Victorian virgin over the possibility of a simple good-night kiss. And she was anything but shy, retiring or an innocent virgin. Not that she was *very* experienced in that direction, but she did have some. She was a thoroughly modern, independent woman, pushing thirty, damn it.

But then, Lisa had more than a hunch that a goodnight kiss from Fitz would be a far cry from simple.

Tension. Mounting. Building. Expanding. Lisa folded her hands on her lap and dug her fingernails into the tender flesh of her palms. Dammit! If they didn't get to Matt's soon, she might be in danger of grabbing and kissing him.

To her grateful relief, at that moment Fitz brought the car to a smooth stop with the passenger door right next to the cleared walkway.

"You don't have to walk me to the door," she said, her hand fumbling to unlock the seat belt before reaching to grope for the door release.

"Lisa." His voice was soft, yet somehow commanding.

She froze, and slowly turned her head to face him. Her mind went blank. Her throat went bone-dry. "Yes?" Little more than an embarrassing croak. Pitiful.

Releasing his belt, Fitz leaned toward her, right hand reaching out to curl around her nape. Slowly, very gently, he drew her close to him, until his mouth was a mere inch or so from hers.

A tremor ran up Lisa's spine, around her neck, to settle in her lips. She could smell him, his own exclusive tangy masculine scent. It was more potent than the wine she had sipped before dinner.

He applied light pressure to her nape, urging her to him, to his slightly parted lips.

"Lisa." A bare whisper of sound; it rang inside her head like a shout.

Raising her trembling hand, she flattened it against his chest, feeling the steady beat of his heart reverberate through her entire being. "Fitz...I..." She lost her voice.

Staring first at her quivering lips, then at her splayed hand against his chest, Fitz lifted his other arm, capturing her hand with his. "Ahh, Lisa, you are so beautiful," he repeated his earlier compliment.

Barely breathing, feeling first cold then heat run relays through her body, Lisa wet her lips in preparation. She wanted his mouth. Needed his mouth. More, she wanted, needed the thrust of his tongue into her mouth. Her eyelids growing heavy, she parted her lips.

Raising her hand, Fitz kissed her fingertips. Her eyes flew open as, closing the scant gap between them, he brushed his mouth over her cheek. Releasing her hand, he reached around her to open the door.

"Good night, beautiful Lisa. Sleep well."

Chapter 5

Sleep well?

Lisa was in a state of near shock when she let herself into the house. Leaning back against the door, she listened to the sound of Fitz's well-tuned car as he pulled away, the sound dwindling as he drove down the driveway. She was so focused on listening, at first, that she didn't notice the still quiet of the house, the dim lighting, obviously left on for her.

What time was it, anyway? Lisa hadn't an inkling, but apparently it was past Matt and David's bedtime. Good. She wasn't up to chit-chat. She couldn't handle a grilling by her sister about where she and Fitz had gone for dinner, whether she had had a good time, what she thought of the tall, teasing, tempting home builder. If she liked him.

Liked Fitz? If wanting to jump his bones, nibble on his lips, duel with his tongue meant she liked him, then Lisa supposed she did. She sighed.

Fitz had kissed her hand and her cheek—if one could call that brush of his mouth against her skin a kiss. Sleep well?

She laughed softly, so as not to awaken Matt and David. It was either laugh or scream in frustration. Her body was trembling. She felt weak, achy, empty, needy. Never having felt this way before, it was a completely new experience for her. Lisa didn't like the feeling.

Suddenly inexplicably exhausted, Lisa shoved her body away from the door and turned off the hall light. Listless, shoulders dropping, she mounted the stairs. Once inside her room, she stood staring into middle distance for a few minutes, and then she did something she hadn't done since her freshman year in college. Undressing, she let her clothes lie where they fell and crawled into bed without cleaning either her face or her teeth. She didn't even bother to slip into a nightgown.

Sighing, Lisa closed her eyes, certain she would lie awake, endlessly replaying the evening in her mind, tormented by the desire pulsing through her tired body.

Sleep well? Hell, in the condition she was in,

she doubted she would sleep at all…damn his gorgeous hide.

She was wrong. She was out mere moments later.

Fitz, on the other hand, was still pacing the length of his house an hour after he had dropped Lisa off at the Macdonoughs'. Not that he hadn't tried sleeping, because he had, for all of five or so minutes. He was hot, even though the house was cool, with the thermostat turned down to sixty-six. He was painfully aroused, even though he had stood under a cold shower for as long as he could take. The shower had helped, as did the coolness of the room on his naked body, but unfortunately, not much.

Lisa. Beautiful Lisa.

Fitz's chest expanded, then deflated on a deep sigh. Never, never, never had he wanted a woman, to be with a woman, make love with a woman as he wanted to be with Lisa.

Distracted, uncomfortable and beginning to shiver in the cool air, Fitz trudged up the stairs and into his bedroom to fling himself onto the bed. Heaving another deep sigh, he stared at the ceiling, at the patterns of diffused moonlight filtering through the long sheer curtains at the windows on either side of his king-size bed.

His thought patterns were as diffused as the light shifting on the ceiling. Was that Lisa's profile forming in one of the patterns? His calming body jerked to life again.

Damn. Go away, beautiful, he silently ordered what looked to him, in the fluid motion of light, to be the outline of her tall, curvaceous silhouette.

Another sigh. Another thought. A startling thought. Had he actually alluded to Lisa that there could possibly be a permanent relationship between them? On the very same day he had met her?

A memory, complete with dialogue stormed into his mind, as clear as a scene from a movie. He and Lisa, seated at the table in the restaurant, parrying back and forth about mutual sexual attraction.

He had said it made the world go around.

Lisa had retorted that she had been led to believe that love made the world go around.

Could happen. The confident sound of his own voice rang in his head, reverberated through his body. *You, me, terrific in bed together, and in love.*

Fitz mulled over the concept in his mind, examined the depths and range of his feelings. He concluded that, hell yes, he had alluded to a permanent relationship between them.

Damned if he hadn't meant it. Strangest of all, he really didn't mind.

Weird.

But he would have to play his hand carefully. Lisa was obviously skittish about any serious relationship. As well, she was one confident, independent woman.

Yeah. He'd have to play his hand—and her—very, very carefully. He smiled. It sounded like fun to him.

His body now calmed by his distracting thoughts, Fitz closed his eyes and fell asleep. He was still smiling.

The next day, Monday, after lunch and at Matt's urging, filled with anticipation and an equal measure of trepidation, Lisa climbed into David's car to drive to the job site and inspect her sister and brother-in-law's house.

Not even to herself could Lisa deny the let-down and disappointment she felt when, pulling into the muddy driveway, she saw no sign of Fitz's truck. There were two other trucks, both marked Fitzhugh Home Builder, but no Fitz.

"Grow up," she chided herself in a mutter. "Stop acting like a coed in the throes of her first infatuation." Reaching for the doorknob, she added, in an even softer mutter, "And stop talking to yourself out loud, before somebody notices and throws a net over you."

Lisa sighed, composed herself and straightened her spine and shoulders all at the same time. Pushing the door open, she stepped inside—and stopped in her tracks.

There were two men, neither one of them Fitz, standing in the foyer—Bill the painter and a man

Lisa had never seen before. He frowned at her. Bill smiled.

"Hi, Ms. Wolfe," Bill said, his smile widening. "I was kinda expecting you. Mrs. Macdonough always came about this time of the day."

The other man turned his frown on Bill, and nudged him with an elbow.

"Oh, this here is Jerry Clouser," he jerked his head at the other man. "He's Fitz's field supervisor."

Lisa and the other man stepped forward at the same time, right hands extended. "How do you do, Mr. Clouser? I'm Lisa Wolfe, Mrs. Macdonough's sister."

Grinning, Jerry grasped her hand. "I figured that, Ms. Wolfe," he said. "God, it's incredible how much alike you and Matt are. Identical twins, huh?"

"Yes." She laughed. "Straight down to the tiny identical moles on our right shoulders."

Jerry was shaking his head. "Like I said, incredible. How does anybody tell you apart?"

She grinned. "Well, right now it's pretty easy. Matt's the pregnant one."

Bill and Jerry both laughed.

"At any other time, not many people *can* tell us apart," she admitted, laughing with them. "Our parents can, of course, and our grandmother. David can...don't ask me how, as Matt and I have managed

to fool our uncles, aunts and cousins on many occasions.''

"I can believe it," Jerry said.

"And I've got to get back to work, and finish the
family room," Bill said, moving away. "Before I
have the boss breathing fire down the back of my
neck."

"Yeah, I gotta go, too," Jerry said, glancing at
his watch. "I've got four more sites before quitting
today." He raised an eyebrow at Lisa. "You want
me to show you around the place before I take off?"

"No, thank you," Lisa said, shaking her head.
"I'll be fine. I'll ask Bill if I have any questions."

"Sure," Bill called from the family room. "I'll
be here for the rest of the day."

"Okay, see you." With a wave of his hand, Jerry
left.

Listening to her boot heels clack on the bare
floors, Lisa checked out the kitchen, living and dining room. Before starting up the stairs, she paused
at the archway into the family room.

"The dining room walls look beautiful, Bill," she
complimented him. "What is the name of that
color?"

"Oh, thank you," he answered, glancing over his
shoulder, his hand holding the paintbrush still as a
rock. "That's sea-foam green."

"Hmmm." Lisa murmured, thinking she didn't

know sea foam had a color, other than creamy white. Oh, well.

She wandered around the house for a half hour, even down to the lower level, to the great room or media room...or whatever they were calling them these days. To her, everything in the house seemed to be progressing just fine...but then, what did she know about building a house? That was Fitz's field of expertise. And, of course, she wasn't simply killing time, hoping he would show up. No, of course she wasn't.

Liar.

Impatient with herself, with her unusual emotional turmoil, Lisa left the house, remembering to call a goodbye to Bill as she was about to close the door behind her.

Despite her agitation, she told herself—several times—that she didn't care that Fitz hadn't put in an appearance, even though he knew she would be there around this time every day. Fitz had been at the house when Matt had asked Lisa to make the daily trips for her.

No. She really didn't care.

Uh-huh.

After lunch, Fitz jackknifed out of his desk chair at least a half dozen times and strode to his office door before catching himself up short.

Not much more than twelve hours had passed

since he had delivered Lisa to her sister's home, and yet he had to restrain himself not to run out to the construction site just to see her, talk to her.

Rushing her wasn't part of his game plan, but damn, sticking to his program was tough, since he ached to see her. See her, hell, he ached to sweep Lisa into his arms and run away with her, be alone with her, make love with her straight through for about a week, maybe longer, come up for air only to shower and take nourishment.

Oh, my Aunt Sally, that would be the closest thing he ever hoped to get to paradise.

Fitz frowned at his wayward thoughts. As if Lisa would let him get away with sweeping her into his arms and running anywhere with her. They had just met. And Lisa was a strong-willed and strong-minded woman.

Better to stick with his game plan.

Dammit.

By Friday, the driveway to the new house was paved, the interior painting was finished and men were there to lay the wall-to-wall carpeting. When Lisa arrived, the men were upstairs, so she did her tour of the lower two floors of the building.

Lisa hadn't seen so much as a glimpse of Fitz the entire week. While she continually assured herself it really didn't matter to her, she felt unusually low and a tad edgy as well.

But that had nothing whatever to do with Fitz. She was midway through her monthly cycle, maybe she was starting PMS. Never mind that she rarely ever suffered from either PMS or cramps.

Lisa was so deeply into her thoughts, and into the great room, media room, whatever, that she didn't hear the sound of a vehicle coming to a stop in front of the house.

She did hear the door open and close, but assumed it was one of the men from the carpet company. She also heard the basement door open, and the solid thud of footsteps on the stairs. Stepping out of the huge built-in storage closet along the back wall, Lisa caught her breath at the breath-stealing sight of Fitz descending the stairs.

Dear heavens, he was one gorgeous, delicious-looking man, even dressed in beat-up jeans, plaid flannel shirt, quilted vest and mud-splattered work boots.

Lisa stood stock-still, staring at him, drinking in the look of him. Fitz had come to a halt at the bottom of the stairs, as still as she was, staring at her. Even with the distance separating them, she caught his scent: tangy, masculine, with just a hint of musty male sweat.

Clenching her hands, Lisa had to fight against a nearly overwhelming urge to run to him, fling herself into his arms, finally taste his tempting mouth.

* * *

Fitz couldn't move. Hell, he could barely breathe. She was so beautiful. Slowly, he let his gaze drift from the top of her golden head to the tips of her designer boots. But it was the in-between view that set his heart racing and his rapidly heating blood surging through his veins and parts south.

He wanted her, right there, right then. Wanted to feel her beneath him on the newly laid carpeting. Wanted to devour her with his mouth, thrust into her with his hard body, feel the thrill of her eagerly arching into his every thrust.

Sweat beaded his forehead. Fitz gave himself a mental shake. Making urgent love with Lisa on Matt and David's brand-new carpeting was not part of his game plan.

"What do you think of the place so far?" Fitz was both surprised and proud of the easy, almost nonchalant sound he had managed to produce from his tight throat.

"I think it's going to be beautiful when it's finished." She smiled; Fitz felt an odd melting sensation inside. "Actually, I think it's already beautiful. You and your crew are to be congratulated, Fitz. I believe Matt and David will love it."

And I believe I love you. Fitz froze inside. In love with her? Naw. How could he be in love with her? He'd known her less than a week. He hadn't even kissed her, not on the mouth, though he somehow knew kissing Lisa would be the ultimate pleasure.

Well, maybe not the *ultimate* pleasure, but he felt positive that kissing her would be the wildly arousing, senses-thrilling build-up to the ultimate pleasure.

But love? How could one thought cause the conflicting emotions of scariness and excitement?

"Fitz?" Lisa frowned at him with a mixture of confusion and concern. He seemed...far away. "Is something wrong?"

"What?" He blinked, as if she had wakened him from a sound sleep. "Oh, no, I'm fine." He gave her a small, self-derisive smile. "I was...er, wallowing in your compliment. Thank you. I'll pass it along to my subs."

"You're welcome." Lisa hesitated, knowing she should leave, longing to stay, if only to be near him, look at him. Never before in her life had she experienced so strong an attraction to a man. She felt like a fool. She hardly knew him, and yet...and yet... An idea popped into her mind, and she mentally shook her head. *Love.* Surely she wasn't falling in love with him? Was she? Never having experienced the emotion, Lisa didn't have a clue. She did have the feeling that she had better get moving. "I really must..." she began, moving forward, only to stop when he interrupted.

"How is Matt?" he asked out of the blue. "I haven't seen or heard from her or David this week."

"Matt's fine. She tires easily, but she's fine." She took another step. Again he stopped her.

"When's she due?"

"Who knows?" Lisa shrugged. "Her due date is in March, but with twins—" she lifted her shoulders once more "—Matt could go into labor at any time."

"No scheduled Caesarean section?"

"No." Lisa smiled. "Her doctor suggested it, but Matt is determined on a natural delivery."

He frowned in quite the same manner as David had when Matt had explained her position to Lisa and their parents. "And if there's a problem?"

"Then the doctor takes control." Thinking there was nothing left to say, she took another step, making her three steps closer to him, when he halted her again.

"Are you free for dinner?" He asked abruptly, startling her. "And up to some dancing later?"

"Yes." Lisa should have felt ashamed of the quickness of her response, but she didn't; she felt unabashedly relieved. "What time?"

"Seven again okay?"

"Yes. Now I must go," she said. Before I lose every shred of control and pride and launch myself into your arms, she thought, grateful he saved her from brushing against him by stepping aside to allow her to pass.

* * *

Dinner was an almost exact repeat of the previous Sunday. Fitz teased her with his low, sensuous voice and practically made love to her with his seductive gaze. Five minutes after they left the dining room of the restaurant, the one he had told her about with a separate room for dancing, Lisa couldn't remember what she had eaten.

Dancing with Fitz, being held in his strong arms, close but not too close, was both heaven and hell for Lisa. The feel of him—the warmth radiating from him, heating her blood, that tangy masculine scent of him scrambling her senses—induced wicked ideas of being alone with him, being held tightly in his embrace, his mouth crushing hers.

Although Lisa enjoyed the dancing, as it had been some time since she had danced with anyone, she didn't protest when Fitz asked if she was ready to leave. Protest? The soles of her feet were itching, no, she was itching all over her body. She couldn't wait to be alone with him.

To Lisa's frustration and deep disappointment, the evening ended exactly like the previous one. After coming to a stop in front of the house, they sat silently for several minutes. Then, resigned, Lisa unlocked her seat belt and turned to the door. And, as before, she heard his belt click and then felt his hand on her arm.

"Fitz...I..." she began. And, mirroring her earlier

move, she raised her hand to his chest, felt the promising pound of his heart against her palm.

"You are so very beautiful." Once again, he caught her hand and raised it to his lips for a chaste kiss on her fingers, then leaning close to her, he brushed his lips lightly over her cheek. "Good night, Lisa. Sleep well."

Sleep well? Again. Feeling as if she had been caught in a time warp, she swung the door open and hurried into the house, relieved to find the house dimly lit and quiet.

Sleep well? Like hell.

To Lisa's dismay, she felt stuck in the same time warp throughout the following three weeks. Fitz asked her out one night a week for dinner, sometimes dancing. It was the same scenario every time he drove her back to the house. "You are so very beautiful." A light kiss on her fingers, the brush of his lips against her cheek and, "Good night, Lisa. Sleep well."

There was only one break in his routine. Once or twice, Fitz telephoned her midweek. Big deal. Well, in truth it was a big deal to Lisa, even though she was just about ready to tear out her hair in frustration. The maddening man made love to her with his eyes, his low, teasing voice. Dammit, would he ever get around to delivering on his unspoken promises?

All these thoughts were revolving inside Lisa's

mind at the end of the first week of February, as she dressed to go out with Fitz yet again for dinner and dancing.

Lisa had offered to curtail her evenings out to be there for Matt, just in case. Calm, unshakable David told her to go and enjoy herself. Matt practically shooed her out, while assuring Lisa she'd be fine with David.

Of course, Lisa realized she could give little help to Matt other than moral support, and if Matt needed more of that there were always their grandmother, Uncle Jake and Aunt Sarah.

So Lisa had continued to go out with Fitz, although she was beginning to wonder why she kept putting herself through the torture of being so near, and yet so far away from him.

The evening ran its course as all the others had. They had a fine dinner at the Mansion Inn, where they had had their first dinner together. They went dancing. Fitz held her close, but not too close. Then the course ran out.

"Are you ready to leave?" Fitz asked, as usual.

"Yes," Lisa answered, as usual.

After they were in the car and on their way, Fitz threw her a curve, an exciting, titillating curve.

"Would you come back to my house with me, Lisa?"

"What for?" She knew darn well what for, she

was simply curious about how he'd answer, if he'd be honest. Fitz was both honest and blunt.

"I want to make love with you." He shot a quick look at her. "And I believe you want the same. Am I right?"

"Yes." Lisa could be every bit as honest and blunt as Fitz. "I want to make love with you."

Set free by their mutual honesty, the moment he closed his door behind them he grinned at her and she grinned back. He grasped her hand, and, laughing together, they ran up the stairs and into his bedroom.

Lisa didn't notice anything about the room except the size of his bed. Still laughing, pulling every stitch of each other's clothing off with frantic abandon, they simultaneously reached for each other and fell to the bed.

They went slightly crazy with the release of suppressed passion. Their mouths clashed together in the most shattering kiss Lisa had every experienced. Their tongues twined and stroked, feeding a fire already out of control. When their mouths parted, their lips found other places to kiss. Their hands explored, searching out every sensitive spot. He caressed her breasts, bringing their peaks to tight arousal.

Lisa gasped at the exquisite sensation, and cried aloud in pleasure as his lips suckled at the peaks, sending fingers of flame into the very depths of her core.

Her hands searching, searching, she found, grasped, stroked the hot smoothness of his erection. He sucked in a sharp breath, drawing her breast deeper into his mouth.

Exhaling, Fitz heaved, rolling her over onto her back. "I can't wait any longer," he said, raggedly, settling his overheated body between her long legs.

Lisa stroked her tongue over his nipple, curled her legs around his waist, and confessed, "I can't, either."

Fitz didn't give way to passion by plunging or thrusting, but instead, slowly, carefully, he entered her, joining his body with hers. *Then* he plunged and thrust.

It was wonderful, Lisa thought hazily. She would never have believed that anything could feel so good. She arched high to meet his body with each thrust, moving faster and faster until she was certain she would expire from the gathering excitement, the growing tension. It went on and on, until she was afraid she'd scream. And then the tension snapped. And she did scream, crying Fitz's name aloud in sheer bliss.

He stiffened at her spasms, then thrusting deeply one more time, cried out her name.

"Beautiful, beautiful Lisa."

Lisa shared his bed, and her body with him throughout the night.

It was after seven in the morning when she returned to the house. At the breakfast table, Matt didn't say a word. David didn't say a word. They just sat there with smug smiles on their faces, obviously trying not to laugh as she helped herself to a cup of coffee and a muffin.

Their former routine was over. Fitz initiated a new one. Every evening of the following weeks, Lisa drove to Fitz's house. They prepared dinner together then went to bed. Sometimes they even slept.

Around 5:00 a.m. on February fourteenth, Lisa and Fitz were in his bed, but they weren't sleeping. Their breathing was just returning to normal after a long, leisurely bout of delicious lovemaking, a bout that had lasted nearly two hours, but had been rewarded by two orgasms each. In total for that night, they had slept about four hours…maybe. The quiet in the room was suddenly shattered by the shrill ringing of the phone on the nightstand next to the bed.

"Matt!" Lisa and Fitz spoke in unison.

Still lying on top of Lisa, deeply embedded inside her, Fitz grabbed up the phone and said, "David?"

"Yes, it's me," David answered in a quavery voice that Fitz had never before heard from him. "It's Matt," he was rushing his words now. "She's in labor. The contractions are still pretty far apart, but I've called the doctor and she said to take Matt to the hospital at once. God, Fitz, I hope there's nothing wrong.'' He didn't bother asking if Lisa was there, simply said, ''Will Lisa come?''

''Of course she will,'' Fitz said, glancing at Lisa in surprise. ''So will I. We'll be there as soon as possible,'' he assured him. ''And I'm sure everything will be fine.''

Fitz slid off and away from Lisa as he hung up the phone. ''Matt's in labor. David's taking her to the hospital,'' he said, heading for the bathroom.

''Well, I figured that out by myself,'' Lisa said, all but leaping from the bed. ''But why did you give me that odd look of surprise?''

He turned in the bathroom doorway to grin at her. ''David was far from calm, in fact he was downright shaken.''

''Wonder of wonders,'' she murmured, pulling on her clothes. ''I'm going to run back to the house to shower and change.''

''Okay.'' He headed into the bathroom. ''I'll pick you up after I've showered.''

''Hurry,'' Lisa said, rushing to the bedroom door.

''I won't even shave,'' he promised, achieving his aim of getting her to laugh.

Less than a half hour later, Fitz pulled up in front of the house. Lisa was waiting for him. They arrived at the hospital in Sprucewood ten minutes later. They exceeded the speed limit by only ten miles.

Asking the night receptionist for directions, they

rode up the elevator to the maternity section. At the nurses station they asked for David.

The nurse came around the counter. "Mr. Macdonough is in with his wife." She smiled. "You're Mrs. Macdonough's sister. She asked me to let them know the minute you arrived. Follow me, I'll take you to them."

Matt was lying on her side, David rubbing her back. She went stiff, alarming Lisa.

"Are you all right? Should I call the nurse?" she asked anxiously.

"No." Matt shook her head and gritted her teeth.

"The pains are getting worse?"

Matt sighed with relief and relaxed. The contraction was receding. "Yes," she answered, her voice hoarse from strain. "And closer together. But it's okay. I've had worse."

"When?" Now Lisa and David spoke in unison.

"When I was shot in the line of duty."

"What!" It appeared to be David and Fitz's turn to speak in unison.

"Matilda Wolfe Macdonough, you have never been shot, in the line of duty or any other way."

"I know." Matt grinned. "I just want to rattle you, take your mind off my pain for a moment." Her smile softened. "Don't worry, Lis," she murmured, twisting around to look at her husband, who was still massaging her back. "You, either, David. I promise you I can do this." She looked at Fitz.

"Thanks for bringing Lisa, and coming with her. I think she needs support more than I do."

Matt kept her promise. It required thirteen hours, enduring a lot of pain, near constant attention by her husband and her doctor, but at 6:05 p.m., she delivered a squirming, noisy five-and-a-half-pound daughter. Her second daughter, weighing in at two ounces more, arrived fifteen minutes later. Exhausted but elated, Matt accepted praise and kisses from David, Lisa and even a grinning Fitz. Less than an hour later, she was sound asleep.

David placed calls to the family members in Sprucewood, and to Matt and Lisa's parents in Colorado. He asked the locals to wait until the next morning to visit. Lisa got on the phone to talk to her parents. They told her they'd be on the first flight east they could get.

The babies were in the nursery for the night. In the morning, their little hospital cribs would be rolled in to their mother's room, to stay there until they went home.

David, Lisa and Fitz, nearly as exhausted as Matt, stood shoulder to shoulder at the nursery window.

"Dear God, they're beautiful," David whispered, like an offering prayer of thankfulness.

"Yes," Lisa murmured, just as thankful, already in love with her twin nieces and feeling an amazing twinge of envy for their mother. Pregnancy and the possibility of settling down in Sprucewood with Fitz were the last things she had been thinking of; she was a career woman. Wasn't she?

"Why are they so red?" Fitz interrupted her thoughts in tones of concern, betraying his ignorance of newborns.

David laughed for the first time all day.

Lisa smiled at Fitz. "Most babies are red for a short time after birth."

"Oh," he said, peering through the glass at the girls. "They're so tiny."

"They'll grow," she assured him, fighting back a laugh.

A teasing gleam flaring to life in his eyes, Fitz looked her up and down. "Yeah, I bet they will."

David exhaled a tired sigh. "I'm beat, and while my wife and daughters are sleeping, I'm going home to grab some shut-eye, too." With obvious reluctance, he turned away from the window. "See you two tomorrow?"

"We'll be here," Fitz answered for both of them.

After David had gone, Lisa shifted her adoring gaze back to the window and the sleeping babies behind it.

"I'm beat, too," Fitz said, in a broad hint. "Are you ready to go home?"

"Mine or yours?" Lisa asked, still gazing at the twins.

"Mine."

"You've talked me into it."

"I'm also starving," he said, draping his arm over her shoulder as they left the hospital.

"You want to stop for something or make something at the house?" she asked, around a huge yawn.

"I vote for picking up a pizza, stuffing ourselves, then following David's example by grabbing some shut-eye."

"I'd rather grab you," Lisa said, without a smidgen of embarrassment. She was making strides in the man/woman word-play game.

"Fine, but after the pizza."

The pizza was delicious. They devoured it as if they were actually starving. They cleared everything away, then made a dash for the bedroom.

"Aren't the girls wonderful?" she asked, fumbling in her haste to unbutton his shirt.

"Yeah," he agreed, unclasping her bra. "But I think I'd rather have a boy."

"Boys are nice, too." She unzipped his jeans, smiling as he shuddered in anticipation. "You're a boy."

He smiled back at her in devilish intent. "Let me show you how boys perform when they've grown into men."

He did, and he did a very thorough—no, spectacular—job of it, too.

Lisa felt completely drained of energy. A smile of

contentment on his face, Fitz snuggled her close to
his side, stroked her back...and front.

Lisa yawned. "Fitz."

"Yeah?" He nuzzled her temple.

She purred like a spoiled kitten.

"Will you be my Valentine?"

Laughing in sheer delight at her, Fitz tilted up her
head and gave her a sweet, heartwarming kiss. "I'd
love to be your Valentine, because I love you...like
mad."

"You do?" Lisa blinked owlishly at him. "How
wonderful, because I just realized that I love you,
too...like mad."

"Good, we'll be madly in love together." He
kissed her again, a blazer this time. "But I still want
a boy."

"I'll do my best." She hesitated, then did something she hadn't done since she was little. She giggled. "But don't blame me if a boy turns out to be
two."

"Can we have them on Valentine's day, too?"

She giggled again. "It'll take some work."

He grinned. "I'll get right to it."

He did, too. Lisa enjoyed every minute of the task.
But they missed the projected date by three days.
Lisa and Fitz were too much in love with each other
and their gorgeous sons to care.

The boys looked exactly like their father.

Fancy that.

* * * * *

Nora's extraordinary Donovan family is back!

#1 *New York Times* bestselling author

NORA ROBERTS

Captivated

The Donovans remain one of Nora Roberts's most unforgettable families. For along with their irresistible appeal they've inherited some rather remarkable gifts from their Celtic ancestors. In this classic story Nash Kirkland falls under the bewitching spell of mysterious Morgana Donovan.

Available in February at your favorite retail outlet.

Silhouette®

Where love comes alive™